ARADIA AWAKENS

Book one of the Ovialell series

by

Tish Thawer

Second Edition
First Printing, 2012
Second Printing, 2017
ISBN: 978-0-9856703-9-9
Library of Congress Control Number: 2012915287

Cover design by Regina Wamba of Mae I Design and Photography
Cover image of woman: © 2010 Bigstock.com/Coka (Paid stock)
Edited by Laura Bruzan

Amber Leaf Publishing, Colorado
www.amberleafpublishing.com
www.tishthawer.com

ACKNOWLEDGEMENTS

To my family: You are my constant source of inspiration. I love you.

To Cortney, my spiritual sister: Thank you for always having my back. And to Karen: Thank you for your time and input, it was needed and very much appreciated.

To my amazing cover artist, Regina Wamba: I couldn't ask for anyone better. Thank you for all you do.

And a special thanks to my spirit guides for bringing me closer to Aradia, and giving me the inspiration and encouragement to tell my fantasy version of her story.

ARADIA AWAKENS

Flaky buttery crust, the rich taste of chocolate, the feel of smooth crème against her tongue. *Mmm…delicious.*

These were the thoughts currently plaguing Aryiah's mind. Pie was her escape. It was her go-to dessert for bad days, break-ups, and fights with her best friend. But instead of being able to indulge in her favorite feel good dessert, she was currently sitting in the goddess' upper throne room, holding the book that announced to all of Ovialell who she truly was.

As she gazed at the hordes of unfamiliar faces, her stomach tightened and her entire body started to shake. Maybe she wasn't ready to *'take her rightful place,'* as everyone kept putting it. The desire to run away from this entire scene threatened to overwhelm her, but just then, a strong hand settled on her shoulder.

My mate, she thought. His touch alone was enough to calm her nerves. The only problem was, his nearness also stirred the wolf she was now able to become.

"My love, I am barely in control right now."

He chuckled quietly, then sent his thoughts into her mind. *"I'm sorry to have rustled your wolf, but listening to your musings about chocolate crème pie and the thought of you licking it from my chest has left me ravenous. I think I'll be reminding you of the idea later."*

A smile spread across Aryiah's face. With this sexy man beside her, she knew she could face anything . . . even her destiny.

Aryiah stood and lifted the now glowing book above her head and the crowd went wild.

CHAPTER ONE

Aryiah shoved her cell phone back into her purse as she and Devin climbed the stairs of her favorite library in her hometown of Colorado Springs, Colorado.

"Who was that?" Devin asked.

"Who do you think?" Aryiah cast a speculative look at her best friend. "My mother, of course. Telling me how *fabulous* her latest trip to Spain was going."

Devin laughed. "Why don't you ever go with her? She's filthy rich and travels the world, while all you ever do is travel from your apartment to work. Why not live a little and join her for once?"

Aryiah passed through the rotating doors of the library then paused and looked back at Devin. "You know me better than that." Her lips barely twitched, unable to produce a real smile.

After her dad's death, Aryiah's mother traipsed around the

world on the money she'd inherited, while Aryiah's childhood consisted of major amounts of time spent with tutors and maids throughout the years. As a teenager, Aryiah had spent hours in this very library researching how to communicate with the dead, desperately hoping to reconnect with the ghost of her father.

Shaking her head, she tried to escape the thoughts of her past as she climbed the main stairs. At the top, Aryiah turned left and came to a stop in front of the massive wooden arch that led into the occult section of the library. The archway was finely crafted, displaying detailed carvings of metaphysical symbols. She entered the room and was flooded with a rush of memories from the time she'd spent here as a teenager. It smelled the same; a light musty aroma drifted from the old manuscripts, and a fine layer of dust shimmered in the rays of light that filtered in through the high windows.

"So, what exactly are we looking for?" Devin asked, pulling Aryiah from her thoughts.

It'd been second nature to invite Devin on this little research trip. After meeting in college, the two of them were joined at the hip. Devin had always been the smartass, wild child of the pair with her flaming red hair, killer body, and great sense of humor, while Aryiah remained the grounded, down-to-earth one. They'd been through so much together, including two weddings. Aryiah was Devin's maid-of-honor, and Devin hers when each of them had gotten married. Now, two divorces later, they were a couple of single women in their early thirties currently standing in the occult section of the library about to research the Wiccan religion.

"Well, I don't know *exactly*, but recently I had a really strange dream and when I woke up, the only thing I could remember was the word *Wicca*." Aryiah looked over her shoulder. "You know I researched this stuff in my past, and with the weird things that have happened to me over the years . . . I don't know, I just feel like it's time that I dove back into it."

With a raised eyebrow and a hint of skepticism in her voice Devin said, "Okay, so do you just want me to start reading and tell you stuff I find interesting, or should I look up the word *superpowers?*" Devin giggled at her own remark.

Aryiah's lashes brushed her cheeks and she purposely held her blink for a few extra seconds. While she loved her best friend dearly, Devin's smartass comments were not what she needed right now. Aryiah's dream truly had felt like a wakeup call—one that left her wanting to pick up where she'd left off in her Wiccan studies all those years ago. So, as much as she wanted to include Devin in this, she knew those who didn't understand the supernatural would have a hard time relating to how serious this subject was to her. Aryiah smiled then shook her head and pointed towards the exit. "Never mind. Why don't you go browse for something you'd enjoy reading instead. I'm sure they have a few Kama Sutra books in the sex section you can use to bone up for your date tonight."

Devin stuck out her tongue and flipped her hair off her shoulders as she followed Aryiah between the tall bookcases. "Maybe, I'll just write my own damn book. With my experience, you know it'd be a best seller." Devin wiggled her brows.

Aryiah laughed and rolled her eyes. "Yes, of course, oh Master of the Ménage."

They both laughed as they wove their way deeper into the back corner of the section. Suddenly, Aryiah stopped and looked over her shoulder with a quick snap of her head. "Hey, did you see that?"

"See what?" Devin asked, looking around from left to right.

"I thought I just saw a woman walking down that aisle."

"Oh shit, are you seeing ghosts again?" Devin's teasing tone came through loud and clear, but Aryiah wasn't kidding. The section had been empty when they came in, but now with the *appearance* of this woman, her senses were on high alert. Turning down the aisle she quickly realized no one was there. *Huh, maybe I am losing it,* she thought, but after a few more steps into the aisle, Aryiah came to a stop in front of a shelf and tilted her head. There were six books lying on their sides as if they'd been laid out on purpose, effectively separating them from the upright ones. She looked at their spines and immediately felt drawn to the texts. Not wanting to give Devin a chance to razz her about her selections, she quickly stuffed the books in her bag.

"Okay. These should do it," she said to Devin, then turned and headed to the checkout counter.

"Hey, are you okay?" Devin asked.

"Yes, I'm fine," Aryiah replied as she picked up her pace. Once they reached the counter, Aryiah set her books out for the attendant to scan, then noticed that Devin was squinting at her with an '*I don't believe you*' expression. Aryiah quickly looked away, then turned to thank the attendant and gasped as she caught the gaze of the beautiful librarian who'd just helped her.

The woman was definitely older than her, but model gorgeous. She was taller than average, maybe 5'9". Her long dark hair shimmered like silk and waved and curled in just the right places. Her sapphire eyes sparkled against the silver silk blouse she had tucked into slate gray pants. Her silver chain belt caught Aryiah's eye; a cluster of small charms—a moon, a star, and a pentacle each hung from a small clasp. Aryiah felt as though time had stopped as her head began to spin.

"Holy shit," Devin blurted. "You guys could be twins. Wow! You're certainly not what I expected a librarian to look like. You look more like the sexy ones you see in the movies with their hair up and glasses on before they whip them off and . . . never mind."

The lady ignored Devin and spoke directly to Aryiah, "Whoa, honey, are you okay? You're looking a little woozy."

7

Aryiah shook her head and focused her attention on the woman. "I'm fine, thank you. You just caught me off guard. I know they say everyone has a twin, but...um, I'm fine. Thank you again."

"My pleasure, and Aryiah, I have another book I think you might enjoy."

Aryiah froze. She wasn't fine. First of all, looking at this woman felt as if she was staring into her own future, and now she was calling her by name and showing an interest in her reading material. No, she wasn't fine at all, she was completely weirded out.

"Um, how do you know my name?" Aryiah stammered.

The librarian smiled and held up something in her hand. "Your library card, of course."

"Ah, of course." Aryiah nodded in acceptance of the woman's response. "As for the extra book, thank you, but I think I have plenty to get me started."

The woman said nothing but stared deep into her eyes and Aryiah's dizziness returned as a faint whisper drifted to her ears. *"You are mine, we have little time, come to me, when you're ready to see."*

The last thing Aryiah saw was the floor rising up to meet her as she fainted.

Aryiah woke on a small chaise in the corner of the library.

"What the hell was that?" Devin was staring down at her with obvious concern. "You scared the crap out of me."

"I don't know," Aryiah said, leaning up on her elbows, "I thought I heard something and then…"

"Well, here. Drink this water. The librarian helped me get you over here and then brought this for you."

Aryiah's head snapped up. That was it; the librarian—something about that woman was why she fainted. She took the water, sipping slowly while she looked around for the woman who truly could be her twin.

"Where did she go?" Aryiah asked, trying for the most casual tone she could muster.

"I don't know, she left the water and disappeared. Maybe she has to report to somebody that her crazy doppelganger with a bunch of Wiccan books just freaked out and fainted in her section."

Aryiah looked up at Devin with scrunched brows and a pout pulling at her lips. "Just because I want to study the craft of the wise, the wheel of the year, and the earth-based pagan traditions that most of today's religions are based on, does *NOT* mean that I'm crazy!"

Devin mouth hung agape as Aryiah sat there shaking. Her frustration wasn't directed at Devin though, but at the fact that for the life of her, she couldn't figure out where all of those words had come from.

"What are you talking about? What wheel, and craft of the who?" Devin looked confused and concerned.

Aryiah felt vulnerable and stupid because she didn't know how to answer. This day was getting stranger and stranger by the minute, and right now all she wanted to do was get the hell out of here. She sat up and gathered her bag. "Just forget it. Let's go. I have to get ready for work."

The two made their way to the front of the library and down the stairs toward the exit. The whole time, Aryiah kept an eye out for the librarian but didn't see her. She felt a sense of relief, but also something else—a sense of disappointment, or loss, perhaps? *How weird is that?* She didn't even know that woman and had never seen her before. But besides the fact they looked so much alike, Aryiah couldn't shake the feeling that the woman was somehow important to her.

Stopping at the front door, Aryiah turned around to take

one last look. She didn't see anyone other than the middle school kids on their field trip, milling around and looking bored. She closed her eyes, leaned her head back, and took a deep breath. As she exhaled, she looked up at the ceiling and noticed a beautiful domed sky light and a perfect white dove backlit by the mid-morning sun. It was sitting on the ledge of the skylight looking straight at her with the most brilliant blue eyes. Aryiah's head started to swim again. *What the hell is happening to me?*

Devin must have noticed her starting to sway and grabbed her elbow, taking her bag. "Come on. Let's get you out of here. I knew overexerting your brain was gonna be a bad idea." Devin laughed nervously then started through the rotating doors.

Aryiah smiled and turned to follow her best friend, but sucked in a breath as she took one last look at the skylight and noticed that the dove had disappeared.

CHAPTER THREE

Aryiah was still shook up during their trip home from the library, and Devin suggested they stop to grab a bite to eat, swearing it would make her feel better. Thank goodness, she was right. Aryiah sipped her herbal tea and nibbled on her blueberry muffin and was finally able to calm down. She listened to Devin talk about what she was going to wear on her date, where they planned to go, and just how she was planning her attack. At that, Aryiah laughed, because *attack* was exactly the right description for Devin's seduction tactics.

"When are you going to stop sleeping around and settle down again?" Aryiah asked.

"Maybe when you do, minus the sleeping around part," Devin answered with a raised brow.

Aryiah hadn't been seriously interested in anyone since her divorce from Pete. She truly never expected to get divorced, though now that she was, she couldn't be happier. She and Pete married young and moved from Colorado to Texas for his job, and Texas is where he started to change. He became very involved in a church that was not of their denomination and started behaving strangely and criticizing her for not being '*religious enough.*'

Aryiah grew up Methodist and attended church regularly. She had, what she thought, was a good relationship with God. She just didn't think she needed to go to a building and listen to someone speak about something she could read about herself, or give that person her money or her car like Pete had. Seriously, he gave away their car as a donation to the church without even talking to her. Things went downhill from there, but luckily Pete moved them back to Colorado before the end.

The breaking point came when she woke up with him standing over her. With a strange look on his face, he raised his arm, pointed at her, and said, "*I see witches rising out of you.*"

She'd sat up and grabbed his arms, trying to shake him awake, but he just jerked away and said, "*I want a divorce,*" then walked out of the room. It was then she realized, he *was* awake.

She remembered feeling surprised but not the overwhelming sadness one would expect. Instead, she felt nervous. Nervous of what it meant and how her life was about to change.

Similar to the feeling she was having now.

Once Aryiah dropped Devin off at her house—a nice little bungalow in the older section of downtown Colorado Springs—she made a bee-line across town to her apartment which was settled on a bluff, high above Garden of the Gods.

Aryiah loved her apartment. It was a two-bedroom one-bath with granite counter tops, a fireplace, and vaulted ceilings. Her home was layered with varying shades of creams, reds, and blacks, with accents of gold and silver thrown in. Her furnishings weren't overly expensive but had nice clean lines and a very contemporary feel to them. *Home sweet home.*

Aryiah dropped her overloaded book bag on the floor next to the sofa. Then, glancing at the clock, realized it was only a little after 11 a.m. and she didn't have to be to work until 2 p.m. She'd already showered that morning for her early trip to the library with Devin, and with how well that turned out... *Yep, time for a nap.*

Aryiah lay down on the couch and pulled the cashmere throw over her and was suddenly struck by an overwhelming feeling of exhaustion. She'd felt worn out before, but not like this. It was as if she couldn't stay awake, even if she tried—like something was pulling her down into oblivion. The moment her head hit the pillow, she was out.

In the darkness surrounding her, Aryiah could feel someone else's presence. She called out, "Hello? Is anybody there?"

No one answered, but catching the sound of movement behind her, she quickly spun around.

The air enveloping her was so thick, it almost felt alive. Suddenly, she spotted the most brilliant pair of green eyes not far from where she stood.

Shit...oh shit, oh shit. She couldn't tell if this was an animal or a person, and she didn't have a clue what to do. But, almost immediately a sense of peace settled over her, and she realized she wasn't afraid.

She took a deep breath and called out, "Hello? Can you tell me where we are?"

"You are in Lower World, my lady, and I am your guide."

Okay, maybe she was feeling a little scared after all. "Um, Lower World? As in Hell?"

"Does this look like Hell to you?" asked the strong voice.

Aryiah looked around as the blackness started to dissipate. She was standing at the mouth of a cave on a cliff's edge that overlooked the most beautiful valley she'd ever seen. Flowers of all kinds covered the landscape. Evergreen trees and lush ferns surrounded a crystal blue lake sparkling in the sun, and on its far shore stood a gray stone castle.

Aryiah quickly turned to find her *guide* then jumped back, covering her mouth with her hand as she stood there in complete shock.

"Well…does this look like Hell to you?" asked the beautiful black wolf with the most piercing green eyes.

CHAPTER FIVE

Aryiah bolted off the couch, tossing her cashmere throw to the floor. The alarm she'd set to wake her up was blaring in the background. She ran to turn it off, realizing it must have been going off for a while, because it was now 1:43 p.m. There was no way she could be ready in time to make it across town to the hotel.

Aryiah was a concierge at an upscale hotel and worked the 2 to 10 p.m. shift. She liked her hours because they allowed her to sleep in, get things done mid-morning, and still go out after work if she wanted to. Not that she did much of that. She lived in the Springs for most of her life, except for the Texas nightmare, so she was very knowledgeable regarding local history and all the touristy things to do around the area. She liked her job and was damn good at it, which made this phone call even more difficult.

Aryiah had never called in sick before, and with such short notice, she wasn't sure how well her boss was going to take it. Unfortunately, there was no denying her dream left her feeling scattered and anxious, almost as though she was forgetting something important. "Yeah, going to work!" she reprimanded herself as she picked up her phone.

"Rochelle, it's Aryiah. Yes, I know I'm usually there by now. No, I'm not on my way. Well, because I'm not feeling very well, and I know that I wouldn't be of much use today. Of course I'll be *of use* by my shift next week. Look, I'm sorry for the short notice, but I fainted today at the library and . . . no, no I'm fine. Like I said, I'm just not feeling a hundred percent yet. Okay, thanks, Rochelle, and again I'm sorry for the short notice."

Yeah, that sucked. Rochelle was crappy at first but then mellowed out when Aryiah told her she'd fainted. *Weird.* It was only a couple of hours ago, yet it felt as if the memory was just out of reach.

Aryiah cleared her head and settled into the fact that not only did she have the night off, but that her next shift wasn't for three days. She was glad she wasn't truly sick, but sure wished she could shake the '*I'm forgetting to do something*' feeling she was currently experiencing. She headed to the kitchen, thinking a glass of water and a couple of aspirin would be the best place to start, but just as she leaned down to pick up the blanket from the floor, Aryiah noticed her book bag lying open.

18

Frozen in shock, she stared at the bag and tried to process how in the hell a bunch of library books could be glowing.

CHAPTER SIX

Aryiah stood staring at the glowing book bag, her mouth open and her eyes wide. A pale green light surrounded the bag, shimmering as if it was made from hundreds of green fireflies. *I must still be asleep.* Aryiah reached out with her right hand and gave her left arm a pinch. "Ouch!" *Okay, definitely awake.*

With curiosity overwhelming her, she bent down to carefully inspect the bag. As she got closer, she realized it wasn't actually the bag glowing, but instead, one of the books inside. As she cautiously reached in to grab the book, she felt a light tingling sensation moving up her arms. It was as if tiny electric shocks were shooting straight into her skin. Thankfully, it wasn't harsh, but instead, a gentle buzzing energy.

Aryiah closed her eyes and reached for the book.

It felt amazing. She laughed as the sensation became a tickle, then removed the book from the bag, watching as the glow subsided. She looked down at the black leather cover and followed the scrolling red ink that read *Aradia or The Gospel of the Witches by Charles Leland*. Her head started to spin again.

"Damn this dizziness." She set the book down, closed her eyes, and took a deep breath. Aryiah hoped that by forcing herself to relax she could shake all the weird feelings she'd been experiencing today. After a few minutes of meditation, she opened her eyes to read the title again.

This time the feeling she got was one of contentment. She opened the book and ran her finger across the page, following along with each sentence as she started to read. It wasn't long before she was engrossed in Leland's words. He described how he came to possess the Gospel, and relayed his take on the Italian *strege*—witches, sorceresses, or fortune-tellers of that time. Then, after the eleven paragraphs of the preface, she came to chapter one: How Diana Gave Birth to Aradia.

It was then Aryiah fainted . . . again.

Aryiah woke to the sound of someone banging on her door. *What the fuck is going on with me today?* she thought as she got up and placed her eye to the peep hole.

Devin's face was staring back at her, scrunched up with worry. She slid the chain off the lock and turned the deadbolt. The second it unlatched, Devin threw the door open and shoved past her into the room. "Are you okay?" She took Aryiah's cheeks in her hands, testing for a fever, Aryiah guessed.

"I'm fine. But how did you know I fainted again?"

"WHAT?" Devin screeched. "I *didn't* know that. I called your work to tell you to get your cell out so you could look at a picture of the outfit I sent you, and *that's* when Rochelle told me you'd called in sick."

"Oh, okay. Yes, I called in sick because I just couldn't get myself together in time to make it to work. I laid down to take a nap and woke up feeling really off." There it was again, that feeling she was forgetting to do something. "Anyway, I'm fine."

"What do you mean fine?" Devin asked. "You just said you fainted again."

"Yeah, I don't know what the fuck is going on with me. After I got up from my nap, I called Rochelle, and then when I was headed to the kitchen, I almost tripped over my book bag..." *Crap, should I tell her about the glowing book?* Aryiah came to a quick decision. *Nope.*

Devin turned and looked at the bag in question, then tilted her head as she noticed the black book lying on the floor. Aryiah's breath hitched in her throat as she wondered if the damn thing was glowing again.

"What's wrong?" she asked Devin. Maybe if she saw the glowing too, Aryiah wouldn't feel like the only crazy person in the room.

"Nothing's wrong. I just thought that book had your name on it for a second."

Aryiah looked down to see what Devin was talking about. *Hmmm.* Aradia and Aryiah did look and sound an awful lot alike.

"Anyway..." Devin said, quickly changing the subject. "I'm glad you're not really sick. Now you can help me finish getting ready for my date."

Aryiah let Devin raid her closet and watched as she changed outfits three different times before settling on a little black dress, strappy black sequin heels, and a light silk scarf to drape over her shoulders. She looked great. Aryiah just hoped everything came back in one piece—she liked that dress.

"I hope it's okay that I told Gage to pick me up here," Devin said. "I didn't know what was going on with you, so I wasn't sure if I'd have time to run home again."

"Totally fine," Aryiah replied. "So where did you meet Gage anyway? You haven't given me the usual run down of your latest victim."

"I've actually known him for awhile. He works with me. I tried to get my claws into him before, but he didn't show any interest until yesterday." Devin stopped primping in the mirror long enough to turn around and shoot Aryiah a serious look. "Which you will not repeat to anyone. *Ever.*"

Aryiah laughed. Devin wasn't used to having anyone *not* show interest in her. Being a bartender in one of the Spring's most popular clubs really helped get her noticed, which was exactly how Devin liked to be—*very* noticed.

Turning back to the mirror, Devin continued. "Anyway, he asked me out yesterday. Actually, he asked *us* out."

"What?" Aryiah exclaimed. "I'm sure I did not just hear that. Who has the balls to ask out two girls at once?"

Devin smiled. "It wasn't exactly like that. It's just that he's seen you there talking to me before, so when he asked me out, he suggested that we double with you and your 'significant other' so there wouldn't be any pressure for our first date."

Devin turned around wearing a wicked smile. "I told him that you didn't have a significant other and that he would like the kind of *pressure* I was thinking of for our first date." She winked and leaned down, grabbing the scarf from the bed. "Hey, this might come in handy later too."

Aryiah shook her head and watched Devin wrap the ends of the scarf around each wrist, giving them a slight tug as if to test their durability. Then, with a playful smile, Devin did a little shimmy before heading to the kitchen to pour the two of them some wine. One hour and a glass and a half later, there was a knock at the door. Devin jumped up to get it, obviously excited to get her night of sin started.

Aryiah rinsed out their wine glasses and listened to Devin greet her prey, then shut the door. "Aryiah, I want you to meet Gage before we head out."

Aryiah rounded the corner, looked up, and came to a dead stop. She'd never seen Gage before, not even at Devin's bar, but she couldn't escape the feeling that there was something off about this guy.

Gage stretched out his hand. "Nice to meet you." His tone was serious but polite.

Aryiah hesitated. She couldn't shake the feeling that she needed to run away from this man, but then seeing the weird look on Devin's face, she reached out and shook Gage's hand, not saying a word. The feeling to bolt intensified. So much so that she jerked her hand back and ran into the bathroom, slamming the door behind her.

She heard Devin giggle nervously. "Please excuse my friend, she's had a really weird day. Let's just go. I can't wait to have you all to myself anyway."

"Bye honey, I'll check on you tomorrow," Devin called out.

Once she heard the door shut, Aryiah finally took a breath.

CHAPTER EIGHT

Aryiah looked into the mirror. Her heart was beating fast, she was pale, and her eyes were dilated.

"What the fuck was that?" she asked herself. She felt bad for embarrassing Devin in front of her date. *Gage.*

Just thinking his name and picturing his face had her shaking again. He wasn't bad looking. Tall, nice body, longer light brown hair, and those dark eyes. His eyes were what freaked her out the most. They were so dark they were almost black.

Taking a deep breath, Aryiah headed out of the bathroom and walked straight to the front door and flipped the locks. She needed to sit down. But as she turned, a bright green glow emanating from the floor caught her attention.

"Oh shit, not again."

She reached down and grabbed the book. But unlike before, the glowing didn't fade. She made it to the couch, sat down, and just stared at the book. Then she heard the voice.

"You were right to run from him."

Aryiah dropped the book and grabbed her knees, folding in on herself. This was definitely the strangest day of her entire life, and it just kept getting worse and worse. *I really must be going crazy. But why?* she questioned, reality setting in. She liked her job, loved where she lived, and didn't have anything in her life to stress her out to the point of craziness. So why was all this weird shit happening?

"Because it's time for you to take your rightful place," the voice replied.

This time she didn't freak out. She was starting to get pissed, so she yelled back, "What the fuck is happening? Who are you and what do you mean, *rightful place?*"

There was a slight pause and then the book lost its glow and the voice continued, "If you are ready to accept your destiny, I will reveal myself to you."

She placed her feet on the floor, readjusted herself on the couch, and straightened her spine. *What the hell, if I'm going crazy, I might as well see what destiny has in store for me.*

After a deep breath, and with a steady voice, Aryiah proclaimed, "I accept my destiny, now please show yourself to me."

A moment later a shimmering green light started to appear in the middle of Aryiah's living room, sparkling just like the light of the book. Aryiah watched, wide eyed, as it grew bigger and bigger, brighter and brighter, until she was staring at a figure forming inside.

"Holy shit!" Not a minute after seeing the green light form, a man materialized in the middle of her living room. A *gorgeous* hunk of a man. He was tall, at least 6'4", tanned skin, dark hair cropped close to his head, and the most fantastic body she'd ever seen. He wore nothing but a pair of black military style pants and matching combat boots. Once she closed her mouth and peeled her eyes away from his amazing abs, she looked up at his face and was mesmerized by a pair of emerald eyes so brilliant, she swore they couldn't be real.

How can any of this be real? she thought.

"Aryiah, don't panic. I *am* real and it's very important that I talk to you," the gorgeous stranger said.

Wait…how did he know what I was thinking? And why doesn't he feel like a stranger?

"Please let me explain. To answer your first question, I know what you're thinking because I can hear all of your thoughts. To answer your second question, I am not a stranger, as we have met before."

Aryiah sat in silence, because right now all she could do was stare. After a few moments of self doubt and thoughts of white padded rooms, she realized he must be telling the truth because those were the exact questions she'd been thinking to herself.

So, mind reading? I can handle this. Since she'd studied all kinds of metaphysical things when she was younger, telepathy and other psychic abilities weren't something she was unfamiliar with. But a man literally appearing out of nowhere in her living room…that was a little hard to swallow.

"You're handling this very well so far," Gorgeous said.

Holding up her hand and shaking her head, Aryiah interrupted. "Before you say anything else, or explain where we have met before—and you *will* explain—what's your name?"

Mr. Gorgeous' smile caused her to melt just a little as he held out his hand. "My name is Damarius."

Aryiah smiled and reached up. She and Damarius gasped at the same time as their fingers touched. As their eyes locked, a warm sensation ran up her arm, through her heart, and straight between her legs.

What the hell is happening? To her surprise, the answer he gave was not out loud, but instead, echoed inside her head.

"Something that shouldn't be possible." He released her hand and stepped back. "I have to go."

Aryiah jumped off the couch and headed to block the door. "You're not going anywhere until you explain all of this!"

His eyes found the floor and he took a deep breath. "I would love to explain everything, but as I no longer understand what's happening, I have to go. I'll return soon to guide you." Then, in a flash of green light and even faster than when he appeared, he was simply gone.

Aryiah moved away from the door, feeling stupid. She forgot that blocking it wouldn't stop him from coming and going. She now stood, stunned, and stared at the spot where Damarius had just been. *"I'll return soon to guide you,"* he had said, then disappeared right before her very eyes. *Eyes . . . those beautiful, brilliant green eyes.* They did seem familiar, and he said they had met before, but she just couldn't place him. "Like I wouldn't remember meeting someone like him," she said out loud.

As she tried to remember all the places she'd recently been and the people she'd met, she bent to pick up the book off the floor and noticed it was open to a page about halfway through the book. It read, *Diana, Mother of Aradia, Goddess of the Witches, Goddess of the Wild Hunt, She Who Runs with Wolves.* Below the sentence was a picture of a beautiful dark-haired woman. She held a bow in one hand, while her other rested on the head of a gorgeous black wolf with the most brilliant green eyes.

CHAPTER NINE

Damarius was shaken. He was finally able to meet Aryiah while in his human form and was still in awe of how gorgeous she was in person. He'd been close to her before as the wolf, her guide through her shamanic journeys in Lower World. But seeing her up close and finally being able to touch her was the most wonderful experience he'd ever had.

So wonderful in fact, that it caught him completely off guard and now he was stalking through the castle of Upper World, looking for answers as to what exactly had happened when he took Aryiah's hand.

Damarius rushed into the throne room looking for his goddess. "My Lady Diana, are you here?"

"I am always with you, Damarius," replied the sweetest voice that had ever graced his ears. The air stirred and he caught the scent of honey and vervain, then the Goddess Diana appeared out of thin air and took a seat upon her throne.

She was so beautiful it almost hurt to gaze directly at her. She radiated a soft silver glow and was dressed in a white gown that crisscrossed her breasts and clung to her waist, then dropped to a puddle on the floor. From the silver chain at her waist hung her athame, as well as a collection of pentacle and moon charms. She was the most stunning woman he'd ever seen. Maybe that was why he was so overwhelmed when he touched Aryiah. She looked so much like his goddess it was unsettling. None of the other women Damarius had ever trained resembled Diana in the slightest.

Damarius bowed then spoke. "My lady, I've made contact with Aryiah, both in my wolf and human forms. She is most...spectacular."

"Did you have any doubt she would be?"

"No, my lady, and even though her memories aren't flowing, it seems she is open to accepting me."

"Time is short, Damarius. Perhaps her memories aren't flowing freely, but her soul is drawn to fulfill her role in this world. Return to her and begin her training. She needs to be ready by the Winter Solstice."

Damarius bowed. "Yes, my goddess, but may I ask one question before I take my leave?"

"Of course. What is it that has you so perplexed?"

Damarius was slightly embarrassed to ask, but he needed to know for certain what had happened when he touched Aryiah.

"When I touched Aryiah's hand, something happened that I've never experienced before."

"Please continue, for now I'm intrigued. What could have possibly taken place that you haven't already experienced during your thousands of years?"

Damarius began to pace as he recalled the experience. "It felt as though I could not leave, could not remove my hand from hers, as though we were being fused together. A warm sensation ran up my arm, straight to my heart." He decided to leave out the part where the sensation continued straight between his legs.

The goddess was silent, but only for a moment. "So, it has finally happened," she said with a loving smile on her face.

"What has happened, my lady?" Damarius begged. He had an idea, but it was impossible, and that left him even more eager to know what this strange connection with Aryiah was.

Rising from her throne, the goddess smiled and walked towards him. She took his hand in hers as she explained. "You have experienced *The Bond*, Damarius. It seems as though you have finally found your mate."

Impossible.

* * * * *

Diana didn't want to share that she too was shocked by the situation. *I hadn't realized how powerful this woman was. Do I dare hope? Could she truly be the one?*

The goddess was confused, which was a rarity in itself. She had sensed when Aryiah was triggered, as she did with every Witch, but the pull she felt toward her had been particularly strong. That pull was the reason she went to the library to present her with the book. But when Aryiah refused, Diana's hopes were dashed. But with this new development, maybe she had been wrong to lose hope so soon.

Only time would tell.

Aryiah straightened up her living room, taking a moment to put the book that continued to fuck with her head back on the coffee table, then headed directly for bed. After seeing the image of the Goddess Diana and the wolf, her brain had shut down. She was on overload and having trouble thinking straight, so sleep was the obvious choice.

The decision was a good one, because she slept so hard it was already ten in the morning. She checked her cell phone to make sure the clock on her nightstand wasn't wrong, but it showed the same time: 10 a.m. While looking at her cell, she noticed she missed three text messages from Devin.

The first read, *"Gage is hot."* Aryiah cringed. The second, *"Dinner was good—me ready for some dessert *wink*,"* Aryiah rolled her eyes. The third message was from this morning, *"Coming over at eleven to give you the replay."* Aryiah sighed and thought, *I need a shower before I can deal with the sex show replay.*

As she headed to the bathroom, she noticed a green light shining from under her bedroom door. *He's back!* she thought, full of excitement.

In the next moment, she heard Damarius' response in her head. *"Yes, I'm back, but if you'd rather experience the replay of the sex show, I can return another time."*

Aryiah was mortified. He heard her thinking about a 'sex show' and thought she was serious. Oh my god, how was she supposed to face him long enough to explain that she was referring to her best friend's nocturnal activities and not some porn obsession she was suffering from?

That's when she heard him snickering on the other side of the door and realized he was teasing her.

Checking her bed head in the mirror and adjusting her breasts so they looked nice and perky in her tank, she pulled open the door and stepped out to face the sexiest man she'd ever met.

"You will NOT read my mind without my permission. ESPECIALLY when I don't even know you're here!" She tried to sound serious and strict, which was really hard as he stood there looking like the definition of a wet dream.

"I do apologize, my lady, it is something that happens naturally when I'm around you. At your request I will make an effort to only communicate out loud." He sounded serious and sad. So sad it made Aryiah's heart ache.

"Thank you, and I'm sorry. I didn't mean to bite your head

off." Aryiah's gaze drifted from his now smiling face down to a white t-shirt that read *Mean People Suck*, the same black, military style pants he had on before, and his black combat boots. The contradiction made her laugh out loud.

"Does my attire strike you as funny?"

Once Aryiah caught her breath she replied, "No. I don't think you look funny, it's just that you talk so proper and old fashioned, yet you dress so…bad-boy normal."

Damarius hesitated for a moment, then replied with a sexy smirk. "Bad-boy?"

Aryiah tilted her head then bit her lower lip. Raking her gaze over him once more, she realized in that instant it was going to be absolutely vital to her existence to find out exactly how *bad* this boy could be. But just as her thoughts were heating up, Damarius' next statement rapidly cooled them down.

"We have to start your training. You have been triggered and there is no time to waste."

Feeling like she just fell down a rabbit hole, Aryiah said, "Excuse me? *What* are you talking about?"

"Please sit, and I'll explain."

He started to lead her over to the couch, but Aryiah had a feeling this conversation was going to take a while. "Wait, I need coffee first." She turned and headed towards the kitchen instead. This would also buy her some time to text Devin and tell her not to come over. The sex show replay was going to have to wait.

After offering Damarius some coffee and having him politely refuse, she settled down on the couch, threw the blanket over her legs, and braced herself for what she was sure was going to be an amazing tale.

As Damarius watched Aryiah prepare her coffee, he thought back to the life changing event that took place earlier in the day.

He was still confused by how he and Aryiah could have shared *The Bond*, which immediately sealed their tie as mates. It should be impossible since she was human and he a werewolf.

But when the goddess had asked, *"Damarius, are you not pleased that after thousands of years you have found your mate, your one true love?"* it only took a moment for him to respond.

"Of course I am, my lady."

He longed for an explanation, but was left confused as he watched the goddess fall into her own thoughts. Upon breaking out of her reverie, she'd said, *"Damarius, return to Aryiah and start her training, and enjoy the fact that you have found your mate. All will reveal itself in time."* Without another word, the goddess disappeared, leaving a light flowery breeze in her wake.

Damarius had immediately shaded back to Aryiah's apartment, and was now ready to begin the daunting task of explaining his world to her.

Once Aryiah took her seat beside him, Damarius began. "Aryiah, what do you know of magick?"

"Well, I looked into some paranormal stuff when I was a teenager, studying all the ways to communicate with the other side. But besides you appearing and disappearing in my living room, and the mind thingy we have going on . . . um, not much else," she answered.

Damarius debated telling her that she could now hear his thoughts because they were mated, but decided it was best to stick to his chosen course of topics. She needed to know the big picture first, so their personal stuff would have to wait. He'd been without a mate for thousands of years, so what was another couple of hours.

"Okay. Well I thought perhaps you were more educated, as you have all of those Wiccan books over there."

Aryiah turned to look at the library books that were now spread out on her coffee table. "I haven't had time to read any of them." Looking unsure, she hesitated then continued, "The only one I looked at was that one," she pointed to the black leather book, "because after I woke up from my nap, it was glowing. So I picked it up, read the title, and fainted, and the only other thing I read was from a page inside—something about a goddess," she finished in a rush.

Damarius knew about the glowing book. It was his doing. But he was still confused as to why it made her faint. He'd only chosen that book to get her attention, as it was the only one in her pile that mentioned the Goddess Diana. He'd hoped that it would jog her memories and give them a head start on her training. Unfortunately, it had not, so he was going to have to start from the beginning.

With a serious look on his face, Damarius began. "A long time ago . . . in a galaxy far, far away . . . "

Coffee went spraying from Aryiah's mouth as she busted up laughing. "Shut up!"

Damarius laughed. "I thought I'd lighten the mood. Maybe now you won't see me as only proper and old fashioned."

In his mind he heard her say, "*Huh. Sexy as hell* and *a sense of humor. I think I'm in love.*"

Damarius tried to show no reaction to her thoughts, as he told her he would no longer read her mind without permission. But at the sound of the word '*love,*' he couldn't help the longing that raced through him. He reached out and took Aryiah's hand and let the warmth wash over him. Just as before, it shot up his arm, through his heart, and straight to his loins.

Damarius jumped up and walked away from the couch, hoping Aryiah hadn't noticed the evidence of his reaction to their mated bond.

"Damarius, what's wrong? I thought you were trying to lighten the mood and now you look so serious."

He was serious . . . in serious need of holding her and kissing her. He wanted to tell her of their bond in that instant, but until she was up to speed and had officially accepted her place and begun her training, he was going to have to let go of such ideas. Knowing that and convincing his body of it, however, were two very different things.

Damarius regained his composure, then settled himself back on the couch. "I'm sorry, I was just considering how to truly begin. I fear that you're going to have a hard time accepting the things I have to tell you."

* * * * *

Aryiah sat quietly for a moment, looking into his eyes. After experiencing the warm sensation that ran straight through her for a second time, the idea of accepting anything this man had to offer had her tingling all over. She couldn't explain why, but she felt as though she could trust him with anything— maybe even her heart.

"Damarius, I'm ready to listen to your story and start my *training*," she said. "And as for accepting all that you have to tell me, I think I've shown I can handle it. You've literally appeared from out of nowhere twice now, and I haven't run screaming for the hills yet. Which, by the way, is exactly what most people would do. So please, can we begin again? I feel like it's time to get this show on the road."

* * * * *

Aryiah was right. Time was running out. The fact that she was feeling a sense of urgency was a good sign. Maybe that meant her memories weren't as buried as he thought.

"My name means Dealer of Death. I have served the Goddess Diana for thousands upon thousands of years. I am charged with the guiding and training of her Witches."

Damarius paused briefly to gauge her response, then continued when she simply nodded.

"In Ovialell, there are many different races, most of which humans believe to be only fantasy. Witches, fairies, vampires, the Amazons, and…even werewolves."

He hesitated to see her reaction to his last revelation, since for obvious reasons, it was of vital importance to him. Smiling, he continued when she nodded and took another sip of her coffee.

"The Goddess Diana rules over them all with the help of the Witches. Diana's Witches are a coven of the most powerful women who run with her during the Wild Hunt. They also protect the citizens of Ovialell with their magick and healing abilities. Whenever a Witch dies, another is called to take her place."

"Okay, wait. I have a question," Aryiah said, shaking her head. "If these Witches are the most powerful women over there in Ovialell, how can they die so easily?"

"A Witch does not die *easily*, Aryiah, or very often. Until recently, I had not been called to train a new one for over 250 years."

"What do you mean, until recently?" Aryiah asked.

Damarius hesitated, debating how much of the current situation in Ovialell he should tell her. He quickly decided it was best to stick to the Witches and the story of their training. "We will get to that, but there's more you need to understand first. When a Witch dies in Ovialell, her replacement is *triggered*. She is sent a dream that directs her to begin her studies of the Wiccan way. Through the Wiccan religion, a Witch develops an understanding of many things—how to ground and center, how to cast a circle and call upon the goddess, and most importantly, how to develop all aspects of her magick."

As Aryiah's eyes widened, he could tell his words had sparked something within her.

"The dream. I had a dream, and all I could remember was the word Wicca. That's why I dragged Devin to the library." After a long pause and a deep breath, she continued. "Damarius, are you seriously saying that I'm supposed to be one of these...*Witches*?"

"Yes, Aryiah. That's exactly what I'm saying," Damarius replied cautiously.

He was expecting her to shut down at this point, or at least start shaking her head in denial. Instead, she just set her coffee down and smiled.

"I can't believe it. All my life I've thought there was something *more* out there. Something *more* inside of me. When my dad died, I spent years looking into the occult, trying to find ways to reconnect with him. And when strange things started happening to me, I just assumed it was because I'd opened myself up to the paranormal. But now, I realize it must have been a part of me all along."

Aryiah threw her arms around his neck. "Thank you for helping me realize that I'm not actually crazy! I can't wait to tell Devin. She's never gonna believe it."

Damarius held Aryiah in his arms as the happiness drained out of him. He knew there was no way to avoid this part—the part that always left these women in ruin. The part where he had to tell them that to become one of the Witches…they were going to have to die.

Devin woke up and started getting ready to head over to Aryiah's. She had to tell her what happened last night, as it was completely unbelievable.

Her date with Gage started out great. He was gorgeous and had a serious *'I'm gonna rock your world'* look about him. But every time she tried to scoot closer to him in the restaurant, or to lean in for a kiss in the car, he just kept pulling away. Remembering the events again, she thought to herself, *What the fuck was that about?*

As she headed to the door, she grabbed her cell phone and noticed the text from Aryiah. "Sorry, something's come up. Don't come over. I'll call you later."

"Oh, hell no…" Devin said as she grabbed her keys and headed for the door.

* * * * *

From his hidden position behind the hedge of boxwood shrubs, Gage watched Devin walk to her car. *I hope she's headed to the Witch's house. I cannot afford to fail this mission.*

His mission was the only reason he asked her out anyway. He'd been sent to find and kill the new Witch the moment she was triggered, just as he had done to all the others. He initially located his target at Devin's bar, but with all the witnesses present he decided to spend his time merely observing her. After understanding the connection between the two women, he knew using the best friend would be the perfect way in.

So, using one of his special talents, he mesmerized Devin into believing he worked there at the bar, and that she had already been interested in him. Then he asked her out, knowing she would say yes.

His plan worked, but when Aryiah proved immune to his mind control, Gage had spent an uncomfortable evening with Devin and was now forced to approach her again, hoping for a second chance to meet his goal. "Hey, Devin. Can I talk to you for a minute?"

Obviously surprised to see him, Devin dropped her keys and gasped. "Gage? What are you doing here?"

"I've been thinking about our date last night, and I feel like I owe you an apology."

He'd been aware of every move she tried to make. She'd been as subtle as a car crash, but he wasn't interested. He'd been too frustrated and annoyed that his plan to kill the Witch hadn't worked.

He was thrilled when Devin called him and told him to pick her up at her friend's apartment for their date. *How much easier could this get?* he'd thought at the time. But when he arrived at Aryiah's apartment and Devin introduced them, that's when things went sideways.

He'd tried to use his mind control in order to convince the Witch to join them for dinner, thinking it would be easy to get her alone and finish her off. But after she shook his hand, she tore herself away and ran to the bathroom. Gage was left stunned and pissed. Nothing like this had ever happened to him before. None of the other potential Witches were able to resist his powers.

"Um, yeah, I guess we can talk. I was just headed over to my friend's again, but I can catch up with her later," she said, after retrieving her keys from the ground.

"No, don't change your plans. I could just go with you. I would like the chance to apologize to her as well. I feel like we got off on the wrong foot for some reason," Gage said with dark eyes.

"Oh, okay. That's a great idea." Devin smiled and then slid into the driver's seat.

They made small talk on the drive over, Gage placating her with an apology about how he'd been distracted during their date. Devin agreed to accept his excuse only if he kissed her at every stoplight, which surprisingly proved to be more enjoyable than he ever would have thought.

As soon as they pulled up to Aryiah's apartment, he hurried out of the car and opened Devin's door. He smiled, finding a twisted pleasure in the fact that this was the second time in two days she had delivered a vampire assassin to her best friend's home.

Damarius didn't have the heart to tell Aryiah about the death rite just yet. He was so filled with a sense of amazement that this woman was his mate, all he could do was sit there and listen to her stories.

"And then this one time when Pete and I were fighting, the horn in his truck started honking outside, and he started freaking out, saying, 'How are you doing that? How are you doing that?' I didn't know what he was talking about until he explained that there was no way the horn should be honking because he disconnected it the week before."

"You're right. It's apparent you've always had magick inside you, and now's the time we draw it out," Damarius said. "Usually when I begin a Witch's training, she has already had some lessons through her journeys, but since you don't remember yours, we will have to begin again."

"Journeys?" Aryiah questioned.

"Once a Witch is triggered, their guide leads them into a series of shamanic journeys starting in Lower World, then up to Middle World, and finally to Upper World, where they meet the goddess. During these journeys they not only face trials, but are given instructions of what they should be studying in the real world in order to prepare them for the release of their magick."

He watched as a sense of clarity settled over her. "That's why I keep having the feeling like I am forgetting to do something," she stated.

"Yes. For some reason, the memories of your journeys aren't flowing, but I'm hoping now that you know everything, we'll be able to unlock them."

Proving his point, Aryiah suddenly gasped. "It was you in my dream—I mean, my *journey*. The wolf with the green eyes. You're my guide. That's where we've met before." The revelation seemed to please her, but apparently left her with even more questions. "Do you always look like a wolf in the journeys instead of yourself? And why can't I remember any of my lessons?"

Now he was nervous. "Actually, Aryiah, there's more I have to explain. It's not only that I *appear* as a wolf in your journeys," he paused, taking a deep breath, "I actually *am* a wolf. I'm the werewolf that leads the Wild Hunt." Damarius felt lighter after the confession; he didn't want to hide any part of himself from her for even a moment longer. Standing up, he moved to the middle of the living room. "May I show you?"

With eyes wide and her mouth hanging open, Aryiah nodded in approval, then watched as he transformed into the huge black wolf she now remembered.

"That's unbelievable!" she said as he shifted smoothly back into himself, clothes intact. "Is that something you can do because of your magick?"

"No. It has nothing to do with magick. I have always been this way. A man who can become a wolf, or a wolf who can become a man, depending on how you look at it."

* * * * *

Their conversation was interrupted by a knock at the door. Aryiah began to move off the couch to answer it when Damarius placed his arm in front of her and shook his head. *"I'm sorry to speak in your head without warning, but there is a vampire on the other side of your door, and I do not want to give any warning that I am here".*

Aryiah was frozen in place. *"Why would there be a vampire at my door and what the FUCK should I do about it?"* she thought back at him, hoping their mind thingy was still working.

Then her heart dropped as she heard, "Hey, Aryiah, I know you said not to come by, but I need to talk to you. Let me in okay?" Devin's voice sounded so normal, and she had been her best friend for years. How the fuck could *she* be a vampire? *"Oh my god, it's Devin. I think I'm going to be sick."*

53

Looking into her eyes and rubbing both hands down her arms, Damrius thought, *"It is not your friend you need to fear. She is with the same one that was here before. The one you ran from."*

"Gage," she thought, now understanding the strange reaction she had to him.

"I told you that you were right to run from him. I'm sorry I forgot to explain upon my return, but…things happened that forced me to place my attention elsewhere at the time."

"Oh thank god, but why is he with Devin?" Aryiah was relieved, but still scared shitless.

"I think I may know, but let's find out for sure. I'm going to disappear…literally. You won't be able to see me, but I will still be here. Just act normal and see what they want. Do not be scared, my love, I won't let anything bad happen to you or your friend."

Aryiah wasn't sure which part of that sentence she liked more, the fact that he wouldn't let anything happen to her or Devin, or the part where he had called her *'my love.'*

After watching Damarius fade into nothingness, she took a deep breath and made her way to the front door. Trying to stay calm, she turned the locks, opened the door, and ushered Devin and the vampire into her home.

* * * * *

Damarius watched from the Shadowlands as the vampire entered Aryiah's apartment. Those with the ability to *shade* were able to hop in and out of it, allowing them to travel shadowed and hidden from the rest of the world. This is also why it appeared as though he materialized out of thin air, when in fact, he was just stepping out of the Shadowlands. All those who ran with the Wild Hunt were able to shade, including the Witches. Vampires, however, did not possess this ability, so Damarius was confident Gage wouldn't be able to sense him here.

* * * * *

"Sorry for dropping by unexpectedly, but I ran into Gage this morning and he wanted to come by and apologize for the . . . um, awkwardness of last night," Devin explained.

Under normal circumstances, Aryiah would be teasing her best friend that she probably *'ran into him'* as she rolled over in bed. But in the current situation the thought terrified her, and therefore, she was unable to find her sense of humor.

"Ummm…okay, but didn't you get my text not to come over this morning?"

"Yeah, but I was heading over *anyway* to talk to you when I ran into Gage, so he hitched a ride. Plus, it doesn't seem like you have anything else going on," Devin said as she looked around the empty apartment.

Aryiah watched as Gage turned to Devin, his eyes going from brown to black as he said, "Devin, why don't you go out and wait in the car? I would like to apologize and speak to

Aryiah alone."

Without hesitation, Devin said, "Okay. I guess I'll go wait in the car and let you guys duke it out alone."

Holy shit! Aryiah couldn't help that her eyes were about to pop out of her head and her chin had almost hit the floor. She knew in that instant that Gage's black eyes meant that he was controlling Devin's thoughts. *"That's how he looked at me last night. I wonder what he was trying to make me do?"*

"I'm wondering why it didn't work," Damarius replied in her head.

As soon as the door closed behind Devin, Gage turned to Aryiah with the same dark eyes and began to walk toward her. "Let's sit down on the couch, Aryiah, where we can be comfortable."

This situation was the furthest from comfortable that she had ever been in her life. "No thanks, I think I'll stand. Besides, you really didn't need to come by to apologize, you didn't do anything wrong. It's just that I had a really weird day and my nerves were shot by the time we met."

Gage halted his approach as a quizzical look fell over his face. As his eyes changed from black, back to their normal brown, Aryiah felt relief, but only for a second.

"I can see that you're truly immune to my gift. That's unfortunate for you as I usually try to make this experience an enjoyable one. But in your case, it looks like we are going to have to do this the hard way." Aryiah listened as she watched a set of fangs extend from his mouth.

An instant before Gage made his move, Damarius appeared behind him in his wolf form. He was ready to spring when Aryiah noticed the large knife Gage had pulled from under his leather jacket. The fear she felt at the possibility of Damarius getting hurt completely overwhelmed her, and in the next second, it was Aryiah's eyes that changed.

* * * * *

Damarius watched the scene unfold as if it were happening in slow motion. Aryiah screamed and then her eyes began to shine like liquid silver. She flung her hands out and a ball of energy engulfed the vampire, completely paralyzing him.

He heard her chant, "I am she who you cannot beat. Retreat from me with goddess' speed. These words I speak you will now heed. Disappear from me, so mote it be."

And then the vampire was simply gone.

Aryiah sat cuddled in Damarius' arms, completely in shock. She hadn't been able to explain how she'd done it, because she truly didn't have a clue. But now that she was remembering bits and pieces of everything, she told him that something like this had happened before in the library, when words flew from her mouth without her even realizing what she was saying.

"I don't like this. What's happening to me? How did I do that? And what the fuck was it that I just did?" She was hoping Damarius would provide her with an answer that explained everything, like, *"Relax my love, you are progressing normally. All new Witches can do that,"* but instead she got the truth.

"I do not understand," Damarius said. "You shouldn't be able to release that kind of magick until after your initiation rite. This is completely unheard of. I must speak with my goddess."

Damarius looked shaken, but there was no way he could be as freaked out as she was, and if he thought he was leaving her here alone right now, he was sorely mistaken.

"Damarius, don't you dare leave me! I have to go talk to Devin. I want to know what happened to Gage, and . . . I'm really scared," Aryiah finished in a whisper.

Damarius pulled her close again, letting her sink against him as tears began to spill down her cheeks. "Sit down, my love. I will go speak with Devin, and when I return we'll try to talk this through."

* * * * *

He didn't know how much he'd be able to explain, but he had to calm her down in order to leave and get answers to the questions that were now plaguing him.

After making her some tea and placing her on the couch, he covered her with her favorite cashmere blanket then made his way out to Devin's car. Realizing they'd never actually met before, made this a bit more difficult than he would have liked. But then again, the vampire wasn't the only one with the power to control someone's mind.

* * * * *

As Devin sat in her car singing along to the radio, she felt a sudden wave of confusion. "What the hell am I doing out here?" It was odd that she was sitting in her car while Gage,

59

who was practically a stranger, was alone with her best friend inside. Definitely not like her.

Just as she got out of her car, she caught sight of a man walking across the apartment's lawn. *Holy hotness.* He was even sexier than Gage and walking straight towards her.

"Hi, are you Devin?" hotness asked.

Caught off guard by the fact that this guy knew her name, she stumbled a bit. "Ummm, yeah. Is there something I can do for you?"

She looked into his eyes, mesmerized by the deepest shade of green she'd ever seen, as he said, "Aryiah sent me to tell you she and Gage worked out their differences but that he had to take off. Also, she isn't feeling well and will give you a call later."

Devin stared at him briefly then said, "Okay, thanks. Tell Aryiah I'll call her later." Feeling a little fuzzy, she got back in her car and drove off. She was happy that her best friend and Gage had worked things out.

Damarius watched Devin drive off then headed back towards Aryiah's apartment. *What a lame excuse,* he thought. Good thing he was a master of the mind-fuck.

Once inside, Damarius asked Aryiah to explain what she'd been feeling and thinking when her outburst occurred.

She explained about the knife and how she didn't want him to get hurt, and about how Gage's mind control hadn't worked on her. She had no idea where the words of magick she spoke came from. This left them both frustrated and confused. But the one thing Damarius could explain was the mind control.

"Aryiah, mind control is a very rare gift, one that only a few in Ovialell possess. The Goddess Diana, myself, and some of the Fae. Vampires, however, are not like the creatures you've seen in the movies or read about in books. Most do not have any special powers at all. They are simply creatures of death that feed, kill, and lurk in the night. It seems, however, that Gage is—was, an exception. He could manipulate minds and walk in the sun. These gifts are, I'm sure, what made him the perfect assassin."

"Assassin?" Aryiah gasped. "Why would anyone want to assassinate me?"

"It's becoming glaringly obvious that you are indeed special. More so than the other potential Witches were, and even more so than I originally thought."

With his heart breaking, Damarius watched her sink into the couch as she asked, "Can't I just refuse to become a Witch and have everything go back to normal?"

"I'm sorry, my love, but there's no going back."

"Why do you keep calling me *my love*? You don't even know me!" She threw off the blanket and stomped into the kitchen. He watched as she traded her tea for a small glass of wine.

Damarius didn't move as she turned to look at him, probably seeing the hurt expression on his face. She then made her way back to the couch and took his hand.

"I'm sorry. It's obvious that I'm not handling this well, but I didn't mean to take it out on you. I actually love it when you call me that," she said. "It's just that I don't understand why, and I don't understand the feelings that we seem to be having for each other since we just met."

Damarius couldn't think of a better time to tell her of their bond. Because honestly, if he couldn't pull her close soon, and kiss away all the hurt and shock that she was feeling, he was going to lose his mind.

"Aryiah, if you feel calm enough to hear it, that is something that I *can* explain."

She settled herself back under the blanket with her glass in hand. She simply nodded and began listening as he explained their mated bond.

"When I first touched your hand, did you feel any unusual sensations?" He tried to gauge her reaction, but couldn't help listening to her thoughts as well. Internally, she was thinking, *"There is no way I can tell him how excited that one touch made me."* So he watched as she simply nodded her response.

Not having the luxury of playing it shy like she was, he continued. "I felt it too. A warm sensation spread up my arms and through my heart, igniting my passion. I was filled with such an overwhelming sense of love and lust for you in that moment that it startled me."

"Oh, thank god. I thought I was a pervert for feeling totally turned on by one handshake. I'm so glad you felt it too," she giggled, her cheeks flushing pink. With that one sentence, the tension eased and he scooted closer as he continued his explanation.

"As I told you before, I can read your thoughts as easily as if you were speaking out loud. I can do that with almost anyone. But the instant I touched you, something changed. Not only could I read your thoughts, but it was as if I could feel them too. I could sense your emotions, and then, when you heard what I was thinking as well, that's when I knew something special had happened."

Even though she sat quietly, he could tell Aryiah was excited. He could sense her emotions, and right now they were a mixture of excitement, hesitation, and major amounts of lust. It was overwhelming and had him feeling as if the timing was finally right.

"I'm sorry that I left so abruptly, but I had to speak with my goddess to gain a full understanding of what happened." He scooted even closer, took her hand, and looked deep into her eyes. "I can't explain how thrilling it was when I received the answer. Aryiah, when I touched you, I experienced *The Bond*. It means that you and I are mates."

It would probably be hard for anyone to understand how after just meeting someone your life suddenly made sense, but for Aryiah, that was exactly what was happening. For only a brief moment had she questioned his explanation, but now she knew it all to be true. She felt the rightness of it in her soul. After everything that happened, this was the one thing that made it all okay. She'd never believed in love at first sight or any sappy crap like that . . . until now. She was sure it had something to do with him being a wolf, because in her world, once wolves bonded they were mated for life.

After experiencing so many strange and unexplainable things, she'd spent years wondering if she was truly crazy. But with Damarius' explanation about Ovialell, the magick now saturating her life, and their mated bond, she knew everything she'd experienced in her life had been leading her to this moment.

Aryiah could sense the relief radiating from Damarius, and it was overwhelming. But it didn't compare to the feelings of fear, love, and lust that were pouring from him as well. He sat quietly after lowering the bombshell that he and she were mates, probably worried that she would freak out. But in this moment, she couldn't have been happier.

She set her glass down, threw the blanket over the back of the couch. "Is it okay if we talk about the rest of this later? I definitely have more questions, but if I don't kiss you right now, I think I might spontaneously combust," Aryiah said with a purr in her voice.

As his lips met hers for the first time, she heard in her head, *"My thoughts exactly."*

The kiss was slow and tender, their tongues barely grazing as she melted against him. As he laced his fingers through her hair, the feel of his strong arms wrapping around her set her soul on fire with a passion she'd never experienced in all of her thirty-two years.

As the intensity of their kiss increased, he ran a hand down her side, taking in her curves. The feel of his strong hand gliding along her body caused her to writhe in his arms as she reveled in his touch.

"Woman, you're going to be my undoing," Damarius sent into her mind. "Aryiah, I've never wanted anything more in my entire life than I want you right now," he confessed aloud.

Feeling as though she too would die if he wasn't making

love to her in the next second, Aryiah let go of all her stress and worry and became lost in his touch. The look of love, mixed with a flare of possessiveness on his face, made her feel like the sexiest woman alive.

They exploded in a frenzy of shredded clothes, kisses, and moans as the passion of their first mating overwhelmed them both. Moments after, Aryiah opened her eyes and froze, taking in the look on Damarius' face.

"Aryiah, I'm so sorry. I'm being summoned."

An instant later she was lying on the couch alone, confused, and completely naked.

Damarius materialized in the throne room of Upper World, right in the spot where the Goddess Diana had summoned him. "What is a vampire doing in my castle?" she demanded.

Damarius was shocked as his eyes found Gage, surrounded by the energy ball that Aryiah had thrown at him. He was still paralyzed, and looked pissed as hell.

Waving his hand, Damarius quickly clothed himself then answered, "Goddess, I can only explain what happened, but I do not have an explanation for why."

He proceeded to tell his goddess exactly what took place in Aryiah's apartment, making sure to relay that after witnessing Gage's unique gifts, he was positive they now held the assassin responsible for the deaths of the other potential Witches.

"What gifts are you speaking of?" she asked Damarius.

"All that I have witnessed is his ability to walk in the sun and control the thoughts of others."

With an intensity that made the hairs on the back of Damarius' neck stand on end, Diana addressed the vampire. "How did you come to possess such gifts?"

Gage just stared at the goddess, refusing to talk.

"Damarius, take him to the dungeon and then return to me. I have much to think about and we have even more to discuss."

With a flick of her hand, the energy ball dissipated and the vampire fell to his knees. Damarius took a hold of his arm and lifted him to his feet, forcing him to shuffle along beside him as they made their way to the dungeons. With the amount of energy that'd been drained out of Gage, he would be no trouble for quite some time.

After depositing the vampire in his cell, Damarius returned to the throne room and found his goddess sitting on her throne, looking sad and exhausted, which was not a look he was used to seeing.

"My lady, are you feeling all right?" Damarius asked, full of concern.

Her shoulders slumped, and she closed her eyes before answering. "Damarius, these last few months have taken a toll on me. I never thought I would again witness such a division in Ovialell. The vampires of Obsidian obviously have a part in it, but there is someone else behind this, someone whose wrath Gage fears even more than my own."

Damarius crossed his arms over his chest. "I too read that

from his thoughts. But who could instill such fear in a vampire and aid him with enough magick to kill Ingrid, therefore triggering her replacement, and why do such a thing?"

"That, too, is something I've been contemplating. As I fear we are facing another very dark time, I will now tell you something that is only known to the Witches and myself."

With a solemn look on her face, the goddess walked down the stairs and came to a stop in front of Damarius. She waved a hand above them both, transporting them directly to her secluded alter room.

"The Witches magick is at its greatest only when they are a complete unit. By killing a Witch, and any of her triggered replacements, you effectively weaken the whole."

Diana took a breath and looked even more forlorn as she continued. "I fear someone has figured that out, and therefore sent assassins to weaken my Witches in preparation for another Great Rift."

Damarius' arms dropped to his side as Diana's words filled him with dread. The idea of another Great Rift was incomprehensible. He hadn't been alive for the previous division of Ovialell, but it was something he knew he didn't want to experience. So many lives were lost during that war, and now, just when he had found his mate, there was more to live for than ever before.

Jolting him out of his dark thoughts, he heard Diana say, "Damarius, I fear we are about to face the Darklings once more."

"Goddess, no!"

The Darklings were a race of beings with extensive magickal powers—the type of magick that could easily give a vampire the power to walk in the sun and manipulate minds. They were humanoid creatures with a thirst for destruction, and were responsible for starting the war that all of Ovialell now referred to as the Great Rift. It was a time when Ovialell was divided between good and evil.

At the time, Diana had the support of her trusted Witches, the Seelie Fae court and their queen, Raeanne, as well as the Amazon warriors and their leader, Kylie.

On the opposing side had been the Darklings, the vampires of Obsidian, the demons of Hel, and the Unseelie Fae court and their ruler, Queen Fayln.

Damarius reflected on all the history he knew regarding the Great Rift, and what was truly disturbing about this was that the Darklings were no longer supposed to reside in Ovialell. They had been defeated and banished to another realm by the most powerful Witch of all—the Queen of the Witches and Diana's daughter...Aradia.

"How do you think the Darklings have managed to break free?" Damarius asked.

"I cannot say for certain, but I'm almost positive that Queen Fayln has something to do with it. I will have to tread carefully while trying to gain as much information as I can without openly accusing her."

Damarius knew Queen Fayln was no match for the goddess, but if Diana was wrong, she'd ignite a feud, and that was something she'd want to avoid since she strived to rule Ovialell with a peaceful hand.

"Damarius, I have also been reflecting on the events you described regarding Aryiah. I feel a very strong pull towards her, and would very much like to meet her. Bring her here through the Shadowlands when the sun sets two nights from now. I feel it's important for us to gain an understanding of what is actually happening with her magick."

Without giving him time to respond, the goddess disappeared. Damarius was honored that his mate was going to meet the goddess even before her training had truly begun. His chest swelled with pride, and as he thought of how he left her, being away was quickly becoming uncomfortable. Unable to keep himself away any longer, he shaded back to Aryiah's apartment, hoping they could pick things up where they'd left off.

* * * * *

Once Damarius left, Diana reappeared and stood at her alter, staring at her personal Book of Shadows. While every witch had one, none possess the powerful magick that hers did. The goddess flipped to the page she was looking for and began to read: *Diana gave birth to Aradia and then set her forth in mortal form to teach her magick to all mankind.*

With everything that had been happening lately, thoughts of her long-lost daughter were occurring more and more often. She had thousands of years to get over losing her during the Great Rift, but now it was as though she was being forced to think of her daily.

"It has to be a sign," she spoke to the book, then listened as it replied inside her mind.

"I am the tomb who teaches all. Aradia's return will prevent the fall. Test the girl and you will see. Present her with me, so mote it be!"

Diana lifted her arms and threw back her head. A silver glow surrounded her, appearing as though she was being hugged by moonlight as she sang out, "I was right!"

As she reveled in the thought of Aradia's return, Diana moved to her cupboard to retrieve the scrying instruments she'd need to start her investigation. There was no way she would be losing her daughter to the Darklings again.

Once seated on the plush pillows that surrounded the low round table located next to her alter, Diana placed a black mirrored bowl in front of her and waived her hand, filling it with water. As the purple candles surrounding the table flared to life, the goddess focused on the still liquid.

It only took a moment before the water began to ripple, and a scene began to appear in the bowl. The goddess watched as a hooded figure, shrouded in mist, hobbled through the darkness. Unfortunately, there were no distinct details as to who or where this *person'* was. Diana continued to watch it meander through the vision until it lifted its head and pierced her with white iridescent eyes.

Startled, she flung the bowl to the floor with a swipe of her hand. Breathing heavily, Diana stood and began to pace. Thick velvet curtains fell into place at her will, covering the tall windows of her tower. She felt as if the being not only sensed her, but could see her as clearly as she'd seen it. She closed her eyes, but she couldn't escape the image that was now etched into her mind. The same image she'd spent thousands of years trying to forget. The milky white stare of the Darklings as they killed her daughter.

CHAPTER EIGHTEEN

As Aryiah lay naked on the couch, feeling satisfied and unsatisfied all at the same time, she was having a hard time believing what had just happened. She had just experienced the most incredible moment with her mate, but was then left alone as he disappeared from sight.

"Aryiah, I'm so sorry...I'm being summoned," he had said. She assumed it was his goddess who had taken him from her, and right now, she would really like to give her a piece of her mind. Slamming her hands into the cushions, she pushed off the couch and headed into her bedroom to redress.

She couldn't stop thinking about the man she would be spending the rest of her life with. He had explained their mated bond to her, and right now, she felt the depth of that connection deep within her bones. As impossible as it seemed, she knew they'd be together forever and she would never want anyone else.

Spent and exhausted, she climbed into bed with thoughts of her mate lulling her to sleep.

* * * * *

Devin was almost home when she suddenly realized...*she was almost home.* "What the hell is going on?" she asked herself out loud. Had she not just been at Aryiah's with Gage? And speaking of Gage, where in the hell was he?

"This is bullshit, I'm not even thirty-five, and I'm losing my frickin' mind." She spun her car in a u-turn and headed back to Aryiah's.

Once there, she ran to the door and beat on it like it belonged to her last cheating boyfriend. "Aryiah, I know you're still here, I see your car. Please open up. I really need to talk to you."

No answer.

Devin tried her cell phone next, texting first, then calling. "Aryiah, what the hell is going on? Where are you? Things are totally freaky right now, and I need you to call me ASAP."

She slammed her cell closed but as she began to turn away, she noticed a green light emanating from underneath the door. *That wasn't there a minute ago.* Now pissed, Devin shouted, "Well fine! If you want to ignore me, I'll just go find Gage by myself."

No telling what freaky Wiccan shit you're doing in there anyway.

* * * * *

Pissed and feeling hopeless, Gage sat in the dungeon cell, weak from the energy ball that had drained him for the last hour and a half. He still couldn't wrap his head around what had happened. *How the hell had that bitch tossed magick like that without even being initiated, and why doesn't my mind control work on her?* he thought to himself. But suddenly, he remembered there was one person who responded perfectly to his mind control—Devin. With a new plan forming, he vowed to use her to gain his freedom, and then that Witch was going to die.

Damarius stepped out of the Shadowlands and into Aryiah's living room once again. The first thing he heard was Devin yelling, "Well fine! If you want to ignore me I'll just go find Gage by myself." *Good luck with that,* he thought.

He waited for Aryiah's response, as it was obvious the two friends had been fighting from the strength of Devin's emotions. It only took him a split second to realize there was no reply. He wondered if Devin had upset Aryiah enough to cause her to storm off.

Damarius eased his way towards the closed door of her bedroom, hesitated, then lightly knocked. There was no response. Now he was getting worried.

The main problem with traveling from Ovialell and back was the time shift. It meant enough time had passed here while he'd been gone that Aryiah could have gotten herself into some serious trouble.

Now panicked, images of her knocked out from an uncontrollable magickal burst, kidnapped by another assassin, or worse, drained by an assassin and lying dead, were flooding his mind.

As he burst through the door, Aryiah shot up from the bed, eyes wide, arms sprawling, and still totally naked.

The relief he felt at that moment was immeasurable. But then again, so was the sense of lust pouring off his mate as she stared up at him with smoldering eyes.

"Welcome back," she said in a husky voice. Aryiah lowered herself back to the bed as Damarius climbed in beside her.

Wrapping his arms around her, he kissed her sweet lips and saw images of chocolate silk pie topped with cherries. Sweet, decadent, and addictive . . . just like her.

Breaking the kiss, Aryiah looked into his eyes. "I want you," she said.

He returned his lips to hers, kissing her deeply again, then spoke into her mind, *"I want you too . . . as you are my heart, and from this moment, we will never be apart."*

A feeling of warmth settled between them, surging and pulsing, then shooting straight to their hearts. Aryiah's eyes flew open as she gasped. "What did you just do?"

With a smile on his face and a serious look in his eyes, he told her, "I've cast a spell that brands us together. Now wherever you are I can feel it here," he said, gesturing to his heart.

Aryiah's initial instinct was to be pissed that he'd done this without her permission, but her thoughts were calmed as he continued to explain.

"Now, not only can you hear my thoughts at all times, but you'll be able to sense where I am by simply concentrating and thinking of me."

Aryiah lifted a brow, and teased in response. "That sounds like something that could come in handy the next time you disappear and leave me naked and alone."

She laughed as Damarius smiled, then claimed his mouth once more.

After a much needed calming bath laced with lavender and chamomile oil, the goddess retired to her bedchambers.

Even though she'd assumed the Darklings were behind the murder of Ingrid and her triggered replacements, seeing one through her vision had left her truly shaken. They were the only beings with enough magick to pose a real threat to her and her Witches.

As Diana recalled the hordes of Darklings that surrounded her daughter in the moments before her death, she reached out and caressed the statue of Aradia that stood on her nightstand, just as she'd done for thousands of years. Her heart was fraught with mixed emotions at the idea of her daughter's return. Yes, it would be a true blessing to have her back, and her return would mean the Witches would be a complete unit once more. But, it also meant her intuition was right, and Ovialell was on the brink of another Great Rift.

With feelings of joy and sorrow settling in her chest, Diana crawled into bed. She'd have to contact Shay, the now Queen of the Seelie Fae, and Kylie, the leader of the Amazons tomorrow and discuss her findings. Ovialell needed to prepare, because the goddess knew the future they were facing would mark another dark time in their world's history.

*****

Zakrill had felt the moment the goddess' gaze fell upon him. He quickly reacted by surrounding himself in mist. There was no way he could let her know that he was actually back on Ovialell.

After her daughter had cast him and his brethren to the lost realm of Abrinthill, a once thriving demon world, they had spent thousands of years recuperating and trying to regain their magick.

After centuries of in-fighting resulting in massive losses to their numbers, the Darklings were given a gift. A portal had opened in the front of the abandoned castle they called home, and out stepped the Unseelie Queen.

Fayln had offered them a once in a lifetime opportunity. The Darkling with the most power, which they'd have to prove by eliminating the rest of their kind, would be able to accompany her back through the portal and return to Ovialell in exchange for helping her gather enough magick to challenge the Goddess Diana.

The dark Fae had always been power hungry, so her request for more magick didn't surprise him. Zakrill proved his worth by eliminating the remaining Darklings, then followed the Queen back to her castle in Karistan on the Middle World of Ovialell as the last of his kind.

After bestowing Fayln with a few new powers, he took his leave with a plot of his own forming in his mind. The idea of taking on the goddess was one he was familiar with. The Great Rift had started because his people wanted to rule Ovialell, much like the Unseelie Fae queen did now. But this time, ruling was no longer his goal. He sought revenge, first and foremost, for their banishment, but now he had a new goal—a quest to rebuild his race.

He would have to start recruiting and therefore fled to the only place he knew to look . . . the Lower World. There, he found his first willing recruit in the vampire, Gage. A simple promise of becoming more than he was and the vampire jumped at his offer. After summoning the dark magick needed to create the perfect assassin, Zakrill was maimed, but if his loss contributed to the rise of the Darklings, it was a sacrifice he'd make over and over again.

CHAPTER TWENTY-ONE

With the loss of energy Gage had experienced he would need a little more time to recuperate before his magick was fully restored. He didn't mind the delay, however, since he had to wait for Devin to fall asleep before he could put his plan into motion anyway. He lay down on the hard cot and let a smile spread across his face as he stared at the sigils that covered the dungeon walls. The idea of the goddess thinking he had no way out was laughable. Day-walking and mind control weren't the only powers the Darkling had bestowed upon him.

Gage closed his eyes, knowing it would only be a matter of time before he'd be free once again.

* * * * *

Devin felt as if all she'd done today was drive back and forth. She had initially headed over to Aryiah's to talk about her date with Gage, but then things had gotten confusing and now she couldn't find Gage anywhere. He wasn't answering his cell and she didn't see him walking near Aryiah's apartment, even though he apparently left without a car. She vaguely remembered meeting Mr. Hotness but didn't have a clue as to who he was or why he was at Aryiah's house. Angry at how her day had turned out and so sick of worrying about Aryiah and all her bullshit, Devin entered her own house a little after 2 p.m., walked straight to the couch, threw herself face down, and closed her eyes.

The moment Devin started to drift to sleep, she began to dream of Gage. She could hear his voice whispering her name.

"Devin, come to me."

"Devin, I need you."

Smiling in her sleep, she opened her eyes and stared into a candlelit tunnel made of cold stone, then again heard Gage whisper her name from somewhere close by. *"Devin."*

Her excitement grew as she inched forward. She wondered how this dank place was going to play into her fantasy, since she was certain that was exactly what this was. But as always, she was ready for anything, and a hot dream was exactly what she needed to ease her frazzled nerves.

As Devin crept forward through the dark tunnel, she noticed symbols placed on the walls every few feet. There were spirals, moons, pentagrams, and odd looking designs that looked like, *Oh what was the word? ...* Sigils. *Hah! I remember some stuff from helping Aryiah,* she thought proudly.

Sigils were symbols based on magick squares that used numerology to transform words into symbols of power. She had no idea what each sigil here meant, but as she got further along the tunnel, she noticed more and more of them littering the walls. As she came to the end of the tunnel, she heard Gage whispering her name again from somewhere to her left. After a few steps around the corner, she started seeing what looked like jail cells. *Mmmm . . . this I can work with.* Sexual energy surged through her veins.

All the cells were empty but one. She found Gage, looking hot as hell, lying on a hard-looking bunk with his fingers pressed to both temples.

After fluffing her hair and adjusting her bra to make the most of her cleavage, Devin called out to Gage using her sexy voice. "Time to wake up and beg for your freedom."

* * * * *

Gage slowly sat up and dropped his fingers from his temples as a satisfied smile spread across his face. *Damn, I love this power.* He had summoned Devin through her dream using a form of dream compulsion. All he had to do was establish a mental connection to someone, then he could call them to his side through their dreams. It was how he stayed fed when stuck in situations like this. *Not that I get caught and imprisoned very often, that's for damn sure.*

As he approached Devin, preparing to tell her how to unlock the cell, she held up a hand and told him to stop.

"Stop right there!" she said. Gage paused. He had learned from experience that it was best to play along with whatever dream his victims thought they were having, as his mind control would not work in the dreamscape.

"Take off your clothes first," Devin said. He stared at her with a sense of dread growing in his chest. He remembered all the provocative moves she tried to pull on their date, but if there was any hope of using her to gain his freedom in this dreamscape, he was going to have to play along. He was annoyed because he really didn't have time to fuck around, no pun intended.

Devin watched as he stripped out of his shirt. "Wow, you're as muscled and sexy as I imagined." She motioned him forward and reached through the bars, rubbing his bare chest.

"Don't you think this would be more fun if I wasn't stuck in here?" Gage asked, hoping to prompt her into opening the cell.

"I think it will be fun with you both in *and* out of this cell," she said as she ran her hand lower.

Gage gasped and stepped back, shaking his head as she started to undress. Unfortunately, his hesitation didn't slow her down. Needing to play this just right and seeing as though freedom was his only goal, Gage wondered what harm could there be? Devin was a beautiful woman, presenting herself in front of him, and he couldn't deny that he was hungry, though now, for two very different reasons.

* * * * *

Devin gasped as Gage reached through the bars and grabbed her around the throat, linking his other arm around her waist and pulling her tightly against the bars. She moaned as he licked the side of her neck, then suddenly felt a sharp pain.

Holy shit, he bit me! Even in her dream, this was a shock. Her usual fantasies were dark and depraved, but somehow, this rough, gothic jail-house scene had her enjoying the release of her dark side even more. She felt sexy and dirty, and suddenly realized that she liked it . . . a lot! *Mmm . . . being bad is fun.*

* * * * *

Gage continued to *enjoy* Devin as he drank from her neck. She tasted so amazing—better than any other human he'd ever drank from. As he continued to feast, he suddenly caught images flashing from her mind to his. This was normal when the connection between vampire and human was this intense. Maybe he would start to date her for real when things got back to normal, as he was truly enjoying himself for the first time in years. Yes, he fed from humans all the time, but none ever tasted this good or had ever been this sexy. And usually, he made it a point not to have sex while feeding, as it could be dangerous. One slip and he'd be the Sire of a new vampire.

Sex while feeding was how vampires were made in his world. Draining the human and then sharing your seed at the time of death was the catalyst for siring new vamps. Whether you were male or female, something about the exchange of both fluids at the same time—death from one, and life from the other was how vampires were created. Gage never thought about it much, because siring a vampire was never something he intended to do.

Just as the thought entered his mind, the images pouring from Devin snapped into focus. She was imagining sexy, dark and dangerous things. With these images flowing between them, the pace of their sexual frenzy increased. He continued to suck from her neck as he didn't want the connection to break and the images to disappear. This was so fucking hot; he didn't want it to end. He loved how wicked Devin seemed in these imagined scenes. She was sexy, powerful, and something else . . . almost evil.

At that thought, he lost control. He released her neck and held onto her as she slumped to the ground.

After being distracted by the best sex he'd ever had, he suddenly realized he was still in the goddess' dungeon. Figuring he needed to continue playing along with Devin's dream in order to escape, he bent down and whispered in her ear. "If I would have known you were this good, our date would have gone much differently. Why don't you turn around, and I'll show you how to open the cell so we can continue this up close and personal."

Devin didn't respond.

Damarius woke up holding Aryiah in his arms. As he kissed her lightly on top of her head, he glanced at the clock that read 4:24 p.m. and realized they had an entire evening, plus the following day before Aryiah was expected to appear before the goddess. He thought about kissing her awake so he could make love to her again, but with as much as she'd been through, he decided to let her rest.

Damarius slowly peeled himself away from her and rose from the bed. As he bent down to retrieve the blanket that had been kicked to the floor, he noticed the edge of a suitcase sticking out from under the bed. He looked at the luggage tag and saw Aryiah's full name for the first time. ARYIAH DE DELOS. *Huh.* Something nagged at the back of his mind, but he couldn't quite put a finger on it. A smile spread across his face. *Aryiah de Delos, soon to be my wife.*

Damarius didn't have a last name and soon Aryiah would

forego hers as well, since after she completed the death and initiation rites, she would be a citizen of Ovialell and no longer a human of Earth. With these thoughts in mind, Damarius got dressed and made his way out to the living room. He needed some time to contemplate how to tell Aryiah exactly what was involved in her becoming one of the Witches.

The death rite was simple enough. After the prospective Witch completed her training, which included her shamanic journeys as well as her Wiccan studies, she would meet with Diana to receive her blessing in the form of a kiss...the goddess' Kiss of Death. And just like that, the Witch died and was reborn as a true citizen of Ovialell. It wasn't painful, but telling someone they had to die was never an easy task.

Disbelief always set in, then shock and refusal, usually followed by panic. Some potential Witches had tried to run from him, some had tried to fight him, but most had simply shut down. But, in the end, they all accepted their rightful place in Ovialell and completed the rites. He hoped it would go smoothly with Aryiah.

After the death rite, the Witch continued to train in the arts of shading and other powers that could only be accessed while in Ovialell. Once these final skills were mastered, it was time for her to accept her place among the Witches.

Every Witch had a different level of power, and therefore was placed accordingly within their ranks. Once a new Witch accepted her position, she was led into the goddess' private chambers to complete the initiation rite. This was a private ceremony, and only the Witches and the Goddess Diana were allowed to attend. *Perhaps this was when the seal of power between the Witches was completed.*

He never considered the possibility that the Witches could have a weakness. They were strong, brave, and caring. Their presence in Ovialell had maintained health, peace, and prosperity for many centuries. But then Ingrid had been killed about six months ago, and all four potential Witches who'd been triggered to take her place had been murdered. It was now obvious that someone had indeed discovered their weakness and planned to exploit it fully. The goddess' revelation had left Damarius shaken. The idea of another Great Rift was unthinkable.

Damarius looked up from his musings and found Aryiah standing in the doorway of the bedroom. She was wrapped in a sheet, pale faced, and looking utterly distraught.

"What's wrong, my love?" he asked as he raced to her side.

With eyes wide and body trembling, she replied in a whisper, "I…I have to die?"

Oh shit. Our bond. How could he have forgotten?

Damarius was used to the fact that for centuries he and his goddess were the only two citizens in all of Ovialell who had the ability to read others' thoughts. The only exception was when someone found their mate and completed *The Bond.*

"Aryiah, I'm so sorry. I was trying to think of a way to

explain all the elements of becoming a Witch to you and forgot that our bond now allows you to hear my thoughts." Dropping to his knees and hanging his head, he reached for her hand. "I'm doing a horrible job as your guide, and an even worse job as your mate. Can you forgive me?"

Aryiah stood there, frozen in fear, but as she looked down at Damarius she could feel the emotions radiating from him: sadness, regret, and strongest of all, the overwhelming sense of love.

"Damarius, you are not doing a horrible job as my mate. In fact, it's our bond that makes all of this tolerable for me. If I didn't have you, I truly don't think I could handle any of this, and I *definitely* know that I wouldn't be standing here contemplating my own death!"

With a sigh of relief, he stood and pulled her into an embrace. "Aryiah, I know this isn't easy for you, but I will do everything I can to help you through it. We'll start your training tomorrow, so you can have a better understanding of your magick, but tonight, I'll answer any questions you have regarding the rites."

Enjoying the feeling of his arms around her, Aryiah returned his hug. "I would like that very much, but first . . . I need food." Wiggling out of his embrace she continued. "I'm going to shower and get dressed, and after that, I'll cook while you talk. I'm pretty sure it's going to take mass amounts of food and wine for me to understand all of what's coming next."

She reached up, took his face in both hands and kissed him before heading to the bathroom.

As Damarius watched Aryiah gather her sheet and head towards her bedroom, he could literally feel his heart expanding in his chest. *Damn that's one incredible woman. How did I get so lucky?*

I was thinking the same thing, Aryiah responded in his head.

He laughed out loud, again surprised by their mental communication. Maybe putting up mental shields would be the first lesson they'd work on tomorrow.

Devin awoke face down on her couch, her body weak and a little cold. She rolled over and stretched like a waking cat. Taking a moment to glance at the large clock on the wall, she realized it was almost 8 p.m., just after sunset. She had to be to work at 10 p.m., so she headed for the shower, flipping the stereo on as she walked past. "Christ," she cried out, covering her ears. "Why is that so fucking loud?" She reached to turn the volume down but saw it was only on level three. *That's weird.* She shook her head and lowered her hands to test the volume again and stared at the stereo as everything returned to a normal level. "Man, I really need to get my head checked out," she said to herself.

The hot water of the shower felt good on her cold skin. She had just enough time to linger and enjoy the relaxing effect as she contemplated what to wear to work. As she started rinsing the shampoo out of her hair, she felt a slight sting as the bubbles ran down the side of her neck. She raised her fingers to examine the area; it was definitely a little tender.

Devin stepped out of the shower, wrapping herself in her favorite fluffy towel. She wiped the condensation off the mirror and gasped. "Holy hell!"

Her skin was pale and her eyes looked like she was coming off a serious bender. As she wiped her hand across her cheek and down her neck, she felt the tender spot again. Leaning in to take a closer look, she saw two dots, kind of like bug bites. *Oh shit, I've been bit by a spider!* That would explain the pale skin and the small puncture wounds.

Devin raced to her computer and opened the page for WebMD and typed in *"How to treat a spider bite."* After searching the links, she followed the directions and washed the bite with soap and water. Then she'd need to place a cold compress on it and take some ibuprofen.

As Devin headed to the kitchen, she was reminded by her growling stomach that she hadn't eaten since breakfast. Figuring she better have something in her stomach so the ibuprofen wouldn't make her queasy, she opened the fridge. "Wow, I really need to go shopping."

She stared at the bleak contents of her refrigerator, then felt her attention being drawn to a white paper package all the way in the back on the second shelf. It felt like it was all she could see, like her eyes were camera lenses that had suddenly zoomed in. Shaking it off, she reached for the item. "Oh, yummy . . . steak!"

Running short on time, Devin popped the steak into a baking pan and shoved it in the oven. While the steak was cooking, she prepared a quick salad and poured herself a glass of red wine. *Mmm . . . Wine makes everything better.* As she watched the clock creep past nine, and knowing she needed to leave in half an hour, she reached in, grabbed the steak, and set the pan on the stovetop. It wasn't her usual medium-well T-bone, but it would have to do, and right now she was starving and it looked and smelled delicious.

After gathering her food, she carried it and her glass of wine to the dining room table. As she started cutting the steak, she watched it bleed out onto the plate. She stared at the oozing steak and felt her heart speed up and beat heavy in her chest. Suddenly, all she could think about was getting this tender piece of meat into her mouth. As the meat hit her tongue and the blood slid down her throat, a sense of euphoria overwhelmed her. In that moment she didn't care if she made it to work or if she ever worked again.

Devin tore at the steak, feeling like a ravenous beast. *Wow, I really need to pay more attention to my eating schedule, I'm absolutely famished.* Once she devoured the delectable meat, she took a couple of deeps breaths and felt her heart rate slow to a normal pace. She finished her salad and sipped her wine, once again able to focus on the task at hand. She put her plate in the sink and swallowed two ibuprofen with the last sip of wine.

Checking the clock again, Devin realized she needed to pick up her pace if she hoped to make it to work on time.

After racing back into the bathroom, she hesitantly looked into the mirror again. Stunned, she turned her face from side-to-side. She already looked better than she had before; her skin color was normal and her eyes didn't look so sunken.

Energy coursed through her, making her feel like she was supercharged. She started applying her makeup, following her usual routine, then took one final glance in the mirror and realized that her eye shadow and liner were a little darker than usual. *Wow! Guess rushing gave me a heavy hand, but damn . . . I look good!*

She ran back to her bedroom and threw open the closet doors. "What to wear, what to wear?" She usually wore jeans, a bright colored crop-top, and her black wedge shoes to show off her great curves. But the idea forming in her head was definitely not the norm. Instead of her usual attire, she grabbed a pair of black leather pants from the hanger in the back of her walk-in closet, then snagged the open-back, black sequined halter, and pulled out her spiked leather boots to complete the look.

Devin stared in the mirror and liked what she saw, even though she didn't really recognize herself at first glance. The image of a sexy redhead, gothed out in black leather and sequins stared back at her, looking good enough to eat.

Feeling sexy, powerful, and full of life, Devin headed to

the living room to grab her keys, taking one last look at the clock to gauge just how fast she'd have to drive so she wouldn't be late. The clock read 9:18 p.m.

"What the hell?" She had only left the kitchen eight minutes ago? No fucking way could she have gotten ready that fast. Make-up, clothes—that always took at least twenty-five minutes. "Whatever. Damn clock probably needs new batteries," she said as she headed out the door.

She figured if she did end up being late, she would just use the over-the-top sex appeal she had going on tonight to talk her way out of another ass-chewing from her boss. Licking her lips as she strutted towards her car she thought, *Sounds like a plan to me.*

CHAPTER TWENTY-FOUR

After showering, dressing, and cooking, Aryiah felt fantastic. She and Damarius had shared a delicious meal and talked all night about the rituals and rites that she would be facing in order to take her place among the Witches.

He'd explained the different species of Ovialell and where each resided, which had been a little confusing at first. He tried to draw her maps to show her where each city was located, but she just couldn't wrap her head around the fact that Ovialell had three different levels.

Damarius had labeled three different pieces of paper, one marked "Lower World," one marked "Middle World," and one marked "Upper World." He then layered them on top of one another, holding them just a few inches apart between his spread fingers.

"Now imagine this is what it looks like," he'd said. "The Goddess Diana, the werewolves, and the Witches all reside in the city of Dalestri on Upper World, while the Amazons live on the island of Themiscyra off its northern shore. The Seelie Fae court reside in Inlavey, and the Unseelie Fae court reside in Karistan, both on Middle World. And lastly, the vampires reside in Obsidian, and the demons reside in Hel, both on Lower World. But when you put all three levels together they make up Ovialell."

She'd shaken her head at the concept, but listened as he'd continued. "While you're still human, the only way to access the different levels is either through your journeys or by using the portals, but once you become a citizen of Ovialell, you'll be able to shade through the Shadowlands just like me."

This piece of information had Aryiah smiling from ear to ear. The idea of being able to *'disappear'* like Damarius had was exciting and something she couldn't wait to learn.

"The goddess has a castle on each level, and we will be living in the one that resides on Upper World in my private quarters."

At the mention of their living together, she took a deep breath and snuggled close to her mate. Aryiah fell quiet as she tried to process exactly how she would fit into this new life. She'd listened to everything Damarius had told her and it sounded fantastic, especially since she knew that they'd be experiencing all these things together. But as she thought about magick, mates, training, and the fact that she'd be meeting a goddess tomorrow night, Aryiah was suddenly very tired. As

Damarius wrapped her in his arms and kissed her goodnight, she realized this was the most content *and* the most unsettled she'd ever felt.

* * * * *

The next morning, after breakfast and coffee, Damarius and Aryiah officially started her training.

"Take deep breaths and clear your mind. Then try to recall anything you can from your journeys," Damarius instructed.

Aryiah did as he said, closing her eyes and breathing deeply, she let herself sink into a relaxed state as she thought about everything that had happened over the last few days. But even though she was now remembering bits and pieces, she couldn't willingly seem to pull them all together.

Her eyes snapped open as she exhaled a sharp breath. "It's not working. Maybe you should put me under or do whatever it is you do so I can go on another journey and see if that helps."

"That's a good idea," Damarius replied. "Now that your memories are starting to flow, maybe taking you back to Lower World will free the rest." Easing her down on the couch, Damarius continued, "Okay darling, just lay back and relax."

As Aryiah lay back and closed her eyes, she could feel the tingle of magick as Damarius transformed into his wolf. It had to be a good sign that she was becoming more sensitive to the magick as it flowed around her.

She felt content and relaxed as she began to think of the last memory she had of Lower World. It didn't take long before she fell into a deep trance, waking to find herself on the cliff's edge in front of the cave mouth just like before. Damarius was there waiting for her, and she was thrilled at how fully aware of everything she suddenly was. *This is going to work*, she thought to herself.

Aryiah felt the magick buzzing in the air, and a sense of peace and power settled over her. She didn't need Damarius to tell her that this would always be the same place where she entered Lower World, she just knew. Just like she knew that the sparkling lake was more dangerous than it appeared, and that the woods were full of creatures that were there to help and hinder her along the way. This was all a part of her lessons and trials. Lessons and trials she could now fully remember.

Unfortunately, all this clarity brought up another problem, one that left her confused and wary. "Damarius, what does this spell do?" she asked as she pulled a piece of parchment from the pocket of the dress she now wore.

Damarius shifted back to his human form then took the paper and stared at the writing. Inhaling sharply, he looked up at her with wide eyes. "Where did you get this?"

"I don't know," she answered, taking a step in his direction. "I just know that I need to read it before I leave here. What does it mean?"

With a furrowed brow and piercing eyes, Damarius backed

away from her. "It's a forgetting spell, Aryiah," he replied coldly.

"What? Why would I have that?"

Damarius crushed the piece of paper in his palm and replied, "I don't know, but we are certainly going to find out." He quickly turned away and disappeared before Aryiah even had a chance to blink.

Back in Aryiah's apartment, Damarius shook her awake and immediately asked, "Do you remember anything?"

She simply stated, "Yes."

CHAPTER TWENTY-FIVE

Gage sat in his cell, fuming and freaking out over how his escape attempt had ended. Not only was he annoyed by the feelings he was obviously starting to have for Devin, but right now, the larger concern was whether or not she was still human.

He'd been so caught up in the moment that he hadn't paid any attention to just how much blood he'd been taking from her. When she slumped to the ground and disappeared before him, he knew she'd left the dreamscape and had woken up in the real world. The problem was, he had no idea what happened after that. It wasn't hard to put the facts together; he'd drank from her while having sex, which for any other vampire meant he'd just become a new Sire. But for him, since he was unlike any other vampire in existence and especially since he'd done those things while using his dream-walking power, he was unclear as to whether it had worked the same or not. *Maybe it's not even possible.*

At that thought, he felt a sense of hope and loss at the same time. He really did need Devin to escape his prison, but now, after their intimate experience, that wasn't the only reason he wanted her. Once he'd started thinking about what it would be like to spend an eternity with her, the idea had consumed him.

"Guess I'll just have to wait and see." If she had been turned, he would only be waiting a little while longer until she came to break him out. Because as a new vampire, Devin would immediately be drawn to her Sire's side.

* * * * *

Devin arrived at work in plenty of time. She parked her car, gathered her bag, and strolled towards the employee entrance with a little extra sway in her hips. When the security guard held out a hand to stop her, Devin shot him a dirty look.

"Damn, sorry, Devin. I almost didn't recognize you," he said, as his eyes bugged out of his head.

"It's okay, Scott. I expect I'll get a lot of that tonight," she replied as she eased past him.

She could almost feel his stare on her ass as she walked into the club. Giggling, she gave herself a little spank as she looked back over her shoulder; just in time to see Scott adjusting himself.

Devin headed straight for the employee lounge to put her things in her locker. The three girls present didn't say anything as Devin walked across the room, but they certainly didn't hide their stares either.

Devin wasn't friends with any of the girls who worked here, so honestly, she didn't give a shit about what they thought of her new look. But, being the nice person she was, she didn't want any work-place drama, so to lighten the mood she thought she'd chat up the girls before their shifts began. As she turned to engage them, she was suddenly overwhelmed with the strangest feeling and all thoughts of small talk were quickly forgotten.

Devin watched as Nicole put her hair up in a bun, something she always did before work, but tonight, Devin couldn't stop staring at her neck. It was long and elegant, porcelain smooth, and twitched slightly in time with her heartbeat.

"Wow, Nicole. You have a really beautiful neck," Devin said.

The look on Nicole's face matched the scoffs she heard from the other girls. "Thanks, I guess," was Nicole's only response. All three girls cleared out of the room as quickly as they could.

Mentally flipping them the bird, she turned towards the mirror to do one final makeup check before clocking in. Startled, she immediately found the reason the girls must've rushed out the door. Her eyes looked completely bloodshot and were a strange shade of reddish-brown, and she literally had a tiny drip of saliva at the side of her mouth. She looked like a ravenous beast.

"What the fuck?" She snatched a tissue to wipe the side of her mouth and grabbed the eye drops from the drawer where they kept the first-aid kit. Maybe she was having some sort of reaction to the extra eyeliner she piled on tonight. Who knows? But right now, she didn't have time to ponder the effects of crappy makeup or she'd be late for her shift.

After checking her eyes again, happy to see them back to normal, she headed for her bar. She wasn't going to let a few stuck-up bitches ruin her night. She felt great, and for some weird reason, the thought of Nicole's neck caused a buzzing sensation in her head. Between that and the thumping music that was making her body sway, she knew she was going to have a good time.

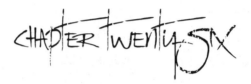

Chapter Twenty-Six

Aryiah rose from the couch and rubbed her head, running her fingers through her long dark hair. Damarius had gone to the kitchen to fetch her a glass of water, but as he walked back into the room, the twitch to his jaw and the hard look in his eyes was proof that something was wrong.

"What do you remember, Aryiah? How did you get that forgetting spell, and why have you been purposely reading it before leaving your journeys?"

She took a sip of water and forced herself to relax. She was trying not to get upset at Damarius' accusing tone, but it was definitely rubbing her the wrong way.

"Damarius, I don't know. I remember my trials, all of them, and how I finished them with ease. My magick flowed smoothly during my journeys and at the end of each lesson, it's as if I was forced to read the spell before returning. I don't understand it either."

Aryiah watched as he paced, splitting her gaze between his worried face and the imprint his shoes made in the plush carpet. "What are you thinking?"

"I think I'm going to kill that assassin, whether my goddess approves of it or not."

"What? You know what happened to Gage?"

"Yes. Your spell encased him in an energy ball and sent him to the goddess' castle in Upper World. That's why Diana pulled me away from you. He's currently in her dungeon, and it's one of the reasons the goddess is eager to meet you."

Aryiah jumped up from the couch and joined Damarius in his pacing.

"Why didn't you tell me? How am I going to explain myself when I don't even know what really happened?"

"I'm hoping that once we show the goddess this forgetting spell, she can pull the memories forward that will help explain exactly what's been going on." Damarius stopped pacing and reached out to take her hand. "Don't worry, my love, I'll be with you the whole time."

Relaxing slightly, Aryiah leaned forward and placed a light kiss on Damarius' lips. "Thank you. That does help. But the idea of not knowing how to explain myself, or what to say in the presence of a goddess is still a bit disconcerting. So . . . do you mind if we try to take another journey?" She watched for a reaction, but continued to speak when Damarius made no response. "If you keep hold of the spell, I shouldn't be able to read it again, plus now that I remember everything about my magick we can test out some things while we're there."

Damarius sighed, obviously debating the logic in her request. "All right. But the minute I sense something strange, I'm guiding you back out."

"Deal." Aryiah quickly reclaimed her position on the couch, and this time she watched as her gorgeous mate transformed into a beautiful wolf right before her eyes. Watching him shade right in front of her had her even more excited to embrace her magick and truly begin her new life.

* * * * *

Damarius watched from the mouth of the cave as Aryiah joined him in Lower World once more.

When she asked to take another journey so soon, he debated whether or not it was a good idea. But with the amount of information she gained from a visit that only lasted minutes, it seemed imperative that they try again in order to gauge the extent of her magick. He'd also been impressed with her bravery of not backing down in light of their discovery.

"Are you remembering still?" he asked.

"Yes. I remember everything that happened so far. I completed my trials in rapid succession and now possess all the magick inside of me. I know how to access it, I just don't understand where it came from."

Damarius stalked forward, feeling the ground shift beneath his large paws. Just as he reached Aryiah's side, he was blinded by a brilliant white light.

Jumping in front of Aryiah and baring his teeth was an automatic response, but when his goddess stepped out of the light, he relaxed and lowered himself to the ground in a show of complete reverence.

"Rise, Damarius, my great wolf." He rose and stalked to her side, then felt the goddess place a hand upon his head.

He heard Aryiah suck in a shocked breath then watched as she too bowed in a show of respect. "It's you. The woman I saw at the library. You're the Goddess Diana. I recognize you from a picture in a book."

Damarius quickly shifted from his wolf form, meeting his goddess' gaze with confusion in his eyes.

"Yes, Aryiah. I'm the Goddess Diana. I presented myself to you at the library as a test. But when you left, I thought I was wrong about my theory. However, in light of recent events, and because I can feel your presence whenever you enter Ovialell, I believe my initial assumption was correct."

Damarius couldn't take it anymore. He blurted out, "What theory? And why didn't you tell me you presented yourself to her before?"

He knew questioning her was probably the wrong thing to do, but he couldn't help feeling protective of his mate, whether it was from a vampire assassin or his very own goddess.

"There are things that even you do not know, my great warrior. But please don't feel slighted, I had to make sure before I shared any of my thoughts with you, or anyone in Ovialell. Please bring Aryiah to my castle tonight as planned, and all will be revealed."

Chapter Twenty-Seven

When Aryiah woke back in her apartment, she didn't need to look at Damarius to see he was extremely frustrated. She could feel the emotion radiating off him like heat from the desert sand.

"Damarius, please calm down. Everything will be all right."

"What, do you know what's going on too? Is leaving me in the dark the way things are going to be now?"

Feeling the intensity of his emotions caused Aryiah to pull her legs up to her chest as she sunk into the couch. After pacing and huffing like a raging bull for a few seconds more, Damarius stopped and looked down at her with sad eyes.

"I'm sorry. I didn't mean to upset you. I can feel that you're just as confused as I am, but hopefully, when we meet with the goddess tonight, all will be revealed like she said."

Aryiah pushed off the couch, finding her voice again. "I hope so, because I want to know what's happening to me. Why am I so different than any other Witch you've trained? And what the hell is this theory Diana mentioned, and does it have anything to do with Gage trying to kill me?"

Plagued with more questions than answers, she made her way to the kitchen and poured herself a glass of wine. She was quickly working herself into a frantic state, so she tilted the glass to her lips and let the calming liquid flow down her throat, then closed her eyes and focused on Damarius' voice.

"I have no idea what the goddess is referring to, as obviously she's chosen not to share her theory with me. But whatever it is, it seems to bring her pleasure, so I hope that it will be happy news for us both."

Aryiah sat the half-empty glass on the counter and walked back to her mate. She put her head on his chest and wrapped her arms around him, hoping it would calm her frayed nerves.

"I hope so, Damarius. Because finding out that I'm mated to a werewolf, getting ready to willingly die, and will be living in a completely different world . . . I hope it's good news, because if it's not, I'm fucking out of here."

She tried to layer her words with humor, but couldn't quite pull it off since this was truly how she was feeling. But in reality, she knew as well as he did that there was no turning back from this path. Vampire assassins, forgetting spells, and whatever other hiccups they met along the way, Aryiah knew this was truly where she belonged. All the strange occurrences she'd faced over the years, and the feelings of being something .

. . more, had finally made sense the day Damarius entered her
life.

* * * * *

Upon returning to her castle in Upper World, Diana
headed straight for her altar. Revealing herself to Aryiah in
Lower World only confirmed her suspicions, and now she
needed to prepare for her arrival tonight.

"Her power is strong, but she still claims to not know
where her magick comes from."

The ancient tome resting on the carved wooden lectern
began to pulse under Diana's hands.

*"Give her the test and she will see, memories of her past will set her
free."*

Diana absorbed the book's words, then left to prepare for
tonight's meeting with a smile on her face.

CHAPTER TWENTY-EIGHT

Devin picked up her overflowing tip jar, straightened her shoulders, and winked at Nicole before strutting back towards the employee lounge.

She sat on the floor counting out her tips, which was required every night after closing. She couldn't help smiling at the overwhelming success her new look had garnered.

Men had fallen all over themselves all night long, trying to jockey a position up to her bar, while right beside her, Nicole had been open and ready to serve. The dirty looks *'little Nicki'* speared her with throughout the evening only encouraged her to shake her ass a little more and smile even wider.

"What the fuck was that all about?" Nicole threw her near empty tip jar onto the counter, then stood hovering with her hands on her hips. "Were you giving away free drinks or what? Cause if you were, Manny will fire you, and I'll watch, laughing as he carts your ass out the door."

In a flurry of motion, money went sprawling across the floor, and Nicole let out a muffled scream. Seconds later, she was lying in a pool of blood, her throat ripped open, her eyes nothing more than glazed over orbs.

Devin was breathing so heavily she was practically panting. She looked up into the mirror and let out a wail that shattered the glass. The shards held an image of a redhead with blood dripping from white pointed fangs.

Devin put a shaky hand to her mouth and felt a sharp sting. Looking at her palm she saw a tiny puncture wound in the middle of her blood-soaked hand. Her panic continued to rise as she heard footsteps outside the door. She quickly gathered her money and flew out the back entrance.

Her mind was a whirlwind as she tried to make sense of what just happened. Tears streamed down her face and her body began to shake as shock set in.

Regardless of whether they blamed her for what happened to Nicole or not, the image of herself with blood-coated fangs was enough to realize she'd never step foot in that bar again. So, leaving her car behind, she ran towards her house at a speed that defied all logic. Minutes later, she slammed the front door and sank to the floor. Heaving sobs wracked her body as she let the confusion and fear pull her under.

* * * * *

"What the fuck is happening to me?" was the sentence currently replaying in Gage's head. He felt it the instant Devin embraced her bloodlust and partook in her first meal of human blood. The questions which plagued him earlier that day were set to rest as he felt the connection of his first sired vampire all the way to his core. Apparently sucking and fucking in the dreamscape did work the same as in the real world after all.

A cocky grin settled on his face as he relaxed onto his bunk. He knew the minute Devin fell asleep it would be the last time she'd do so in her world, because when she woke, she'd be a full citizen of Ovialell. She'd wake within his home in the city of Obsidian, as every new vampire woke in the den of their maker. And with the built-in need to locate their Sire, he knew it wouldn't take her long to find him in the goddess' dungeon since she'd be immediately drawn to his side.

Gage shivered at the thought of getting out of this cell and completing his mission. With Devin now a vampire, the idea of watching her kill her best friend was a seductive shot of adrenaline. He reached between his legs to adjust himself as he imagined Devin's fangs buried in Aryiah's neck.

After trying on her fifth outfit, Aryiah turned to Damarius with a scowl on her face. "Stop laughing at me."

Damarius couldn't contain his snicker. "You looked fine in all of them. I know you're nervous, but for the love of the Fae, just pick one already."

"Hey! You may be used to being in the presence of a goddess, but I'm not. This is a big deal to me, and I don't want to screw it up or look inappropriate."

With a set jaw and a crease to his brow, Damarius eased off the bed, his muscles flexing as he wrapped her in his arms. His words were reassuring, but it was the depth of his kiss that drove his point home. "There is nothing you could wear that would seem inappropriate, because it's you, Aryiah. You're what's special."

Relaxing into his embrace and enjoying the rise of passion their kiss was causing, Aryiah let go of her fears. He was right.

This meeting wasn't about how she looked, but instead, about who she was.

She broke their kiss and looked up into Damarius' love-filled eyes. "Thank you. That's exactly what I needed to hear."

As she spun around in his arms, she looked into the mirror once more and was suddenly overwhelmed at the sight of them together. The image of them as a couple had her heart racing and the lust in his eyes mirrored exactly how she was feeling.

She continued to stare at their reflection as Damarius reached up and slowly slid the blazer off her shoulders. As the material dropped past her arms, she felt his breath on her neck. Tilting her head to give him better access, Aryiah moaned and closed her eyes.

His tongue flicked just under her earlobe as she felt him start to work on the pearl buttons of her silk blouse. She opened her eyes when Damarius' mouth left her neck, and watched as he unbuttoned her shirt, revealing her lace demi bra.

The feral look on Damarius' face and the action of his tongue slowly swiping over his lips had her shivering under his attention.

Neither spoke as he removed her blouse, the silk causing her skin to break out in goose bumps as it slid down her back.

She closed her eyes again and reveled in the feel of his touch. His fingertips grazed the top of her breasts as he reached across her, his hand coming to rest in her hair. She leaned into him as his other hand slid down her rib cage, across her stomach, and to the hem of her thigh-high pencil skirt.

Instead of unzipping and pushing it down as expected, Damarius grabbed the hem and lifted, working it up slowly with one hand until it was gathered around her waist.

"Open your eyes," he whispered.

She followed his instructions and was struck by the sensual picture he'd created. With stiletto heels, matching lace bra and panties, the skirt gathered at her waist, a flow of dark chestnut hair, and curves that most women would die for, the image of herself wrapped in his arms was like an electric shock to her system.

Her breathing picked up and she quivered, thankful his other arm was still firmly wrapped around her to hold her in place.

"Damarius, I want you . . . now." She continued to watch their reflection in the mirror as he gathered strands of her hair into his fist, lifted them, and slowly leaned toward her neck. Aryiah moaned as his light kisses turned into sensual swipes of his tongue. Damarius stared into her eyes through the mirror's reflection as he continued to undress them both. The predatory look on his face sent chills up her spine. "I can't wait any more," Aryiah stated.

Damarius' responding growl caused his chest to vibrate against her back. Reaching for her hand, Damarius guided her to the bed. Crawling atop it, Aryiah was on all fours when Damarius grabbed her hips, joining them as one. The ecstasy—

just as overwhelming as their first time—had them both falling to pieces within minutes.

Aryiah felt thoroughly claimed by her mate. Her skin tingled at the feral growls she still heard coming from Damarius. As she began to pull away in an effort to turn herself around, the tingling sensation increased to a level that captured her attention.

Still on all fours, she now faced Damarius as a green sparkling light surrounded her entire body. "What's happening to me?" she asked.

Damarius stood watching as she felt a wave of magick roll over her skin. When she tried to speak again, all she heard was a low growl.

As Aryiah raised her head to look at Damarius, she caught sight of movement in the mirror behind him. Tilting her head for a closer look, she saw Damarius' exquisite backside in all its naked glory, and a beautiful silver wolf standing on her bed.

CHAPTER THIRTY

"My God, Aryiah, you never cease to amaze me. How is this even possible?" Damarius stood naked while looking down at his mate, who was now the most beautiful silver wolf he'd ever seen.

"Don't worry, baby. You'll shift back as soon as you can calm down." He knew she was probably nowhere near calm but hoped his words would help. "I don't understand how this is possible, but since we are headed to meet the goddess, I'd say this is reason enough to leave early. I'm sure she'll be able to shed some light on what's happened."

Damarius quickly dressed as Aryiah paced around the room on high alert.

He knew what it was like to experience the world in wolf form. She was probably sensing things she'd never noticed before. The feel of the carpet under her paws, the intensity of the light shining from the overhead fixture, the sound of the swirling blades from the ceiling fan—all amplified to a level of extraordinary detail.

He approached her with firm steps and ran his hands across her soft pelt. She lifted her head and huffed through her nose. He could tell she was pissed, but he couldn't help being awe-struck.

"I have to continue to touch you in order to take you through the Shadowlands as we shade to the goddess."

Upon hearing his words, Aryiah pressed close to his leg. He pulled her tight and immediately shaded into the goddess' chambers.

"My lady, we are in need of your guidance," Damarius called out, patiently waiting while stroking Aryiah's fur.

The shimmering light and gentle breeze that flowed into the room announced Diana's presence.

"Oh my!" was her stunned response to Aryiah's current form.

"My goddess, please explain how this could have happened. While Aryiah is my mate, she is human, and this miraculous event has left us both shaken."

Diana approached Aryiah without fear, then knelt and gently wrapped her arms around her. Damarius watched as Aryiah rested her head on Diana's shoulder as the goddess stroked her back. Within seconds the green light pulsed and Aryiah shifted back to her human form.

Aryiah rose from the floor while trying to cover her

nakedness. "And here I was worried about what to wear." They all laughed at her attempt to diffuse her embarrassment. The goddess waved her hand in the air, graciously providing a stunning white robe that wrapped around Aryiah's body. Bowing her head, Aryiah simply replied, "Thank you."

"I'm so glad you're both here, as it's obvious the time to discuss your magick is upon us." The goddess gestured to the alcove beside her throne. "I'm sure what you've just experienced was a complete shock to you both, but I believe I have an explanation."

Damarius squeezed Aryiah's hand as they parted the white gauzy curtains that surrounded a small sitting area filled with all white furniture. He continued to hold her hand, trying to provide a small measure of reassurance that everything would be okay as they took their seats and listened as the goddess continued. "But first, I have to present Aryiah with something that will solidify my theory."

He felt Aryiah tense up, but he was relieved when she relaxed as the goddess picked up a large leather-bound book from beside her seat. The tome looked as ancient as he was, and he could feel a strong magickal current emanating off it from where he sat.

"This is the second time you've tried to give me a book." Aryiah smiled as she scooted to the edge of her seat.

The goddess chuckled and inclined her head. "I assure you, Aryiah, you have nothing to fear. Simply take the book and let's see what happens."

The anticipation clearly etched on the goddess' face had Damarius' nerves firing in rapid succession.

Aryiah took a deep breath then reached for the book. They were all left speechless as the air in the room whipped to a crescendo.

The goddess smiled, practically beaming, as she nodded at Aryiah to open the book.

As Aryiah slowly lifted the heavy cover, the silver light that poured from the book caused them all to squint. Damarius watched, amazed as the book suddenly came to life.

The pages began flipping themselves and a voice resonated from within. *"Aradia awaken, for you are she, returned to us by the powers that be. Strong and reborn she resides within. Embrace your role as beloved daughter again."*

* * * * *

All was made clear at the book's proclamation. Aryiah's mind was flooded with the knowledge that she was Aradia reincarnated—the daughter of the Goddess Diana who had been sent forth to teach the mortal world of her mother's magick. She was Queen of the Witches, and the one who died putting an end to the Great Rift.

Aryiah looked up at Damarius and felt a sense of love and connection radiating from deep within her soul. "My darling.

Let me explain," Aryiah said as she handed the book back to her mother, who sat silently as tears filled her eyes. "I now understand why we were able to become mates, and why I can transform into a wolf. I, Aradia, was the one who created your race just before I died, as a way to protect my mother and all of Ovialell in my absence. I knew one day I'd return, a day when I was needed again, and from the moment I was reborn as Aryiah, I had a connection to my magick and to you . . . the leader of my wolves."

Damarius remained silent as he listened to her explanation. "It was I who put the forgetting spell in my pocket and made sure Aryiah read it each time before she left her shamanic journey. I couldn't let my power escape before it was time, or things would have been thrown wildly out of balance. I hope you can forgive me."

She reached out to run her hand down his cheek, but was stunned when he pulled away.

"Damarius, what's wrong?"

He ran a hand through his hair as he stalked away from where they were seated.

"I'm sorry, but I don't know how to deal with this. You say things like I, Aradia, yet call yourself Aryiah in the same sentence. It's confusing, and I don't know how I'm supposed to see you now. Are you my mate, Aryiah, or are you the Goddess Aradia returned?"

"I am both. I am your Aryiah, but I'm fully aware that I'm

also Aradia reincarnated. Her magick flows freely within me, because it *is* me. Please." she pleaded, reaching out her hand.

His jaw flexed. "Stay and reconnect with your . . . *mother*, and I'll be in my quarters when you're done." Damarius retreated from the throne room, taking a piece of her heart with him.

Defeated, Aryiah sunk into the plush white couch and looked at her mother for guidance. "I thought he'd be happy now that everything has been revealed."

"Don't lose hope. He never knew Aradia was the creator of his race, and now that you have your memories back, he probably feels like he's lost the only part of you he's ever known. It's going to take some time for him to adjust."

The goddess rose from her seat and Aryiah did the same. She embraced her mother and tears spilled down both of their faces.

Diana pulled back and gazed lovingly into her eyes. "My daughter. I'm so glad to have you returned. When you were triggered, I was immediately drawn to you, and when I saw your last name on that library card, I was simply overjoyed. 'De Delos' means *from* Delos, which is the island where I was born. But when you denied my Book of Shadows, I lost hope it was you. Little did I know that Aradia's memories were already causing you to purposely forget your lessons. You're my daughter from before, but you are Aryiah in this lifetime and that is the identity you need to embrace."

"Thank you, Mother. I can't put into words how strange it feels to have full recollection of my past while still living in the present. But I know that with you, and hopefully Damarius' help, I'll be able to find my way in this new world and take my rightful place by your side without losing myself in the process."

As soon as the words left her mouth, Aryiah started to feel the conflict rising within. She meant what she said; she could recall her life as Aradia as clear as if it had just happened: the war, how she banished the Darklings, the piece of her soul she used to create the wolves. But she could also remember the last time she gave a personal tour of the Garden of the Gods for her job, and when she thankfully talked Devin out of going to Las Vegas to see the Thunder from Down Under.

The melancholy she was feeling must have been written all over her face, because the goddess reached out and gently ran the back of her hand down Aryiah's cheek. "I know you feel lost, that's why it's imperative to embrace who you are now. Let the memories from your past and the power you've gained be nothing more than a way to create a bright future for you and Damarius."

"Thank you. I'll certainly try." Hugging the goddess again, Aryiah closed her eyes and let the maternal feeling of her mother's embrace engulf her.

Damarius paced around his chambers, his steps falling heavy on the white marble floor. His home, high atop the goddess' castle, spanned an entire wing of its own. The gray veined marble covered every surface from floor to ceiling, including the columns that framed the hall which led to the bedrooms.

He scanned his surroundings, looking for a distraction, his focus landing on the door to the guest room—a room he rarely had use for. It was furnished, of course, with the finest things that showcased his masculine taste. But now, with the idea of Aryiah sharing his space, he wasn't sure if what he chose would be comfortable for a woman. Especially a woman who suddenly felt like a stranger.

He stomped to the door and pulled it open. The wooden bed, as well as the matching dresser and armoire, had been intricately carved by the fairies of Inlavey. The tan walls with their ivory and green accents gave it a natural, earthy feeling . . .

or so he thought.

The fact that he had no idea if Aryiah—or Aradia—would like it hit him hard. He slashed his hand through the air, his magick instantly changing the look of the room.

His jaw flexed as he looked upon the new scene. It was no longer a reflection of him, but a mirror image of the bedroom in Aryiah's apartment.

Swiping his hand through the air again, he now saw a lavish Victorian-inspired room with a long chaise, a lace and fringe draped lamp, and a green velvet settee, with a matching arm chair and ottoman.

His shoulders sagged as he shook his head and swiped his hand through the air one last time. The room returned to its original state as he turned and slammed the door.

He stomped across the hall and entered his master bedroom. The burgundy and gold accents shimmered against the black splashes of color throughout. Snapping his fingers, the gold wall sconces burst to life, bathing the room in a soft orange glow.

Damarius peeled off his shirt, tossed it on the bed, and headed for the bathroom. A nice hot shower was bound to relieve the tension currently tying his muscles in knots.

He opened the glass door to his large sandstone tiled shower and slowly turned the gold knobs. Zoning out as he watched the droplets of water fall from the multiple shower heads to the floor, he kicked off his boots and unbuckled his belt. As steam started to gather, he shed the rest of his clothes, taking a moment to stare at his naked reflection in the mirror.

Frustrated he was here alone without his mate—a mate, who in a cruel twist of fate was once again a stranger to him—he stepped into the shower with even more tension radiating from his body.

He dropped his head and rolled his shoulders, the feeling of the hot water running down his neck and back helped to calm him, if only slightly. He didn't *want* to be upset with Aryiah. He understood that none of this was her fault, but the feelings of loss and distance her instant epiphany had created between them weren't going to be easy to shake.

Damarius had never spent much time thinking about his creation. He'd immediately claimed his place as leader of the wolves and protector of the goddess the instant he was formed. It's simply who he was. But with the revelation that Aradia had created him, he wondered if Diana had known all along, and if so, why hadn't she told him. All these questions caused an anger to rise within him, an anger that bordered on depression. Thousands of years of doing his duty, and this was the first time he questioned who he really was.

He quickly showered himself, hoping these depressing feelings would follow the suds straight down the drain.

After drying off, he dressed in blue jeans, a plain navy t-shirt, and his sturdy boots, then headed for the living room. He walked straight towards the floor to ceiling bookshelves that lined the southern wall, and within seconds of scanning the books he located the tome he was looking for. Stalking to the couch, he sunk into its cream leather cushions, opened the cover, and began to read *Aradia or The Gospel of the Witches by Charles Leland.*

After the prologue and the first chapter he slammed the cover shut. *Why am I even bothering with this?* It wasn't as if by reading this book he would suddenly understand Aryiah better. Yes, he might learn about *Aradia's* experiences, but it wasn't the ancient goddess who captured his heart and triggered their mating . . . or was it?

Dammit, how can this work out when I don't even know who I'm in love with?

Damarius tossed the book onto the glass coffee table, rose from the couch, and started pacing once more. After a few strides he heard a light knock on the door.

He took a deep breath, stalked to the massive oak entrance and reached for the handle, already knowing Aryiah was on the opposite side of the door. He could feel her energy radiating straight through the thick wood.

As he turned the knob, he felt as though not only was he opening the door to his home, but one to his heart as well. Aryiah stood there, looking beautiful and confident, and his feelings of confusion and conflict instantly disappeared.

"Hi," she said.

He couldn't reply with spoken words due to the lump

forming in his throat, so instead he apologized in her head by thinking, *"I'm so sorry I left you earlier. It was selfish of me to wallow in my confusion or feel like this was going to be hard on me, when it's you who just had the life altering experience."*

Aryiah threw herself into his arms and buried her head in the crook of his neck. *"It's okay,"* she thought. *"I'm at peace with what transpired, but it's the thought of losing you that has my heart feeling as if it's being torn to shreds."*

Using their mated bond to communicate only helped solidify that they were meant to be together.

Their hug quickly turned into a kiss, and Damarius figured if Aryiah wasn't confused about who she was, then he wouldn't be confused by it either.

After breaking their embrace, he led her to the couch. "How did things go with the goddess?" he asked, letting go of his previous questions and anger.

"Good. We discussed the rituals and rites for when I take my place with the Witches on the Winter Solstice."

"The people will be happy to know you've returned and will be taking your place as Queen of the Witches." The stunned look on Aryiah's face stopped him cold. He watched as panic filled her eyes and her chest started to heave.

"I didn't think about that. I'm not sure I want everyone to know I'm Aradia reincarnated. What if things are different this time? What if I don't live up to what they remember?" She shook her head and continued. "I don't think I can handle some grand ceremony."

Damarius took her hands in his and tried to think of something reassuring to say. But honestly, he wasn't sure what it meant to have Aradia return. His initial thought was that it must be a bad sign she'd been awakened after all this time. The thought of his goddess' earlier words drifted through his mind––Darklings, vampire assassins, another Great Rift. How was he supposed to sooth his beloved mate when he was filled with so much concern himself?

He started to speak, hoping the goddess would guide his words, when suddenly their reunion came to an abrupt halt.

Devin woke slowly, stretching like a zombie rising from the dead. Her skin was stretched tight over what felt like brittle bones. She opened her eyes to find herself surrounded by complete darkness. But after a quick blink she was able to focus on her surroundings—her strange surroundings—with perfect clarity.

She instantly recalled what had happened at the bar and smiled as ran her tongue across the tip of her fangs. She knew what she was and what she'd done and reveled in the thought. The only thing currently confusing her was not knowing *where* she was.

She was in what looked like a studio apartment. The floor she was currently sprawled out on was covered in smooth black tile, and the low-lying bed next to her was nothing more than a mattress thrown on the floor, covered with black and gray sheets. The surrounding surfaces looked like slabs of black onyx. Everything was high quality and black upon black: the kitchen counters, the cabinets, the satin wallpaper, everything. So much black—she liked it.

After looking around the open space, she knew she was alone. She stood and felt a surge of strength flow through her entire body as she walked towards the window. Peering out, she sucked in a sharp breath. The sky was a swath of inky blackness, lit only by *two* blood red moons. However, Devin didn't have time to contemplate her odd surroundings because the overwhelming desire to flee was so strong, it felt as if a magnet was pulling her into the night. She opened the door and raced into the darkness, her instincts her only guide. Using her vampire speed, she flew down paved streets, between tall concrete buildings, and ended up in what looked like the center of town.

There was a large circle of grass surrounded by a knee-high stone wall, with openings every four feet. There were people lined up in rows, waiting to enter at each opening.

Devin walked up to the closest line and took her place at the back while staring wide-eyed at a shimmering portal floating in the middle of the grass circle.

She quickly realized that all the people surrounding her were vampires, as a group exited the portal with blood still dripping from their fangs. Devin watched, trying to learn the system. One vampire would return and then another would move forward from a line, enter the portal, and simply disappear. As her line began to move, Devin reached out and tapped the small female vampire in front of her on the shoulder. "Excuse me. How exactly do the portals work? This is my first time."

The woman turned and scanned Devin from head to toe with her beady eyes. Devin tried to plaster what she hoped was a friendly smile on her face, but the woman's chuckle only confirmed her failure.

"You just think of where you want to go, and the portal will transport you there."

Well, shit. Devin didn't have a clue where she wanted to go. Only an overwhelming desire to reach . . . somewhere. "Thank you," she responded flatly.

A few seconds later, it was Devin's turn. She walked forward towards the silver glowing liquid that reminded her of mercury. Upon closer inspection, it seemed to be encased in some sort of metal circle which hovered just above the ground, waiting to engulf her.

Standing within inches of the device, she closed her eyes, took a deep breath, and cleared her mind. Almost immediately a name drifted into her head . . . *Gage!* She stepped through the portal with his face etched in her mind and excitement charging her blood.

As soon as she felt a change in temperature, Devin opened her eyes. She was standing in an open space, the portal now at her back. The green grass was lush, and the tall trees surrounding her created only one way out. The stone path that led away from the portal was lit every few feet with tall elegant torches burning with what she curiously recognized as eternal flames.

Information was starting to free flow into her mind, and she was suddenly hit with the realization that vampires weren't usually permitted in Upper World. Quickly flying from the path, Devin wound her way through the thick evergreens instead. Despite her newfound sense of panic, she tried not to worry about being caught in the goddess' realm.

After only minutes of racing through the forest, Devin could sense she was close to her destination. Slowing, she crept to the edge of the trees, looking for the stone path once again. But what she found instead had her gasping for breath.

A castle so glorious she found herself gaping at the sight. It was simply the most awe inspiring structure she'd ever seen. Pure white marble with shades of pink and silver threaded through the walls like veins of a spider's web. Spires so tall they blocked out portions of the moon-lit lavender sky. White crystal domes topped multiple towers, and walls with repeating arches reminded her of the aqueducts of ancient Rome.

Devin squatted close to the ground as she tried to process the fantasy-like scene. As beautiful as the castle was, she had a feeling if she continued down this path, the fantasy could quickly turn into a nightmare. But unfortunately, the pull she felt towards the stone palace was unrelenting. She somehow knew she'd find Gage within, and the knowledge had her practically flying towards a side entrance she spotted at the far end of the closest wall.

She reached the small wooden door within seconds and yanked it open, completely pulling it from its hinges. Prepared for an attack, Devin bared her teeth and waited, but was pleasantly surprised when she found the hall dark and empty. Listening intently, she heard padded footsteps rounding a nearby corner and leapt into action before they closed in.

The desire to reach Gage was like a beacon in the night, guiding her through hallways, around twists and turns, and finally down a massive set of stairs which led to a candlelit tunnel made of cold stone.

As Devin crept forward through the dark tunnel, she noticed sigils etched into the walls every few feet. The sense of déjà vu slammed into her gut as she rounded the corner at the end of the hall. She spotted Gage standing with his head down and his arms behind his back in the all too familiar cell.

"I've been waiting for you."

CHAPTER THIRTY THREE

Gage rubbed his hands up and down his arms as he tried to alleviate the buzzing sensation coursing through his veins. He could almost sense Devin's every move, and the closer she got to the castle, the more intense the tingling became.

The connection of a Sire to their created vampires was always strong, but when emotions such as lust or love were involved, the supernatural link that bound them together was even more powerful.

Gage shook his head at the ridiculous thought. *Love?* No way. He could admit lust was definitely an emotion currently plaguing him, but love . . . make that no *fucking* way.

He rose from the hard bunk and stood in the middle of the cell, his hands behind his back and his head bowed. He couldn't wait to be free of this place, but the idea of seeing his first sired vampire definitely had him on edge.

He felt Devin round the corner and come to a stop in

front of the cell. "I've been waiting for you," he said.

"You've drawn me here. How?"

"I think you know the answer to that, Devin. I am your Sire. The one who turned you into a vampire. That bond is what drew you to my side, as you are now my responsibility."

"Your responsibility? Why do I get the feeling that pisses you off?"

He slowly raised his head, planning to pierce her with a hard stare and explain that creating a vampire was a burden he never wanted. But upon seeing her here in the flesh, his composure quickly crumbled.

"Dammit, woman. Take a look around," he said gesturing to the cell. "I'm locked in the goddess' dungeon, so can we please get the hell out of here before we start the vampire Q and A?"

Devin planted her hands on her hips and cocked her head and smiled, revealing her fangs to him for the first time. He swallowed hard. She was even sexier than before, and the thought of answering her questions suddenly became the last thing on his mind.

Memories of their shared passion had him running his hands up and down the cold metal bars of the cell. She must have been following his train of thought because she watched his hands stroke up and down, sucking in a breath as though the image stung her.

"What do I have to do?" she asked.

Regardless of what her motivating factors were—sex, answers, whatever—Gage was pleased with her willingness to help him escape.

"Turn around and look at the symbols on the wall. I'll tell you which ones to touch and when," he answered.

While his magickal training with the Darkling had definitely been *intense*, he was currently pretty damn happy he was taught to read sigils. Deciphering them to make his escape would be easy, but since these sigils were wards as well, he needed Devin to actually touch them in a specific order, therefore activating their magick to release the cell doors.

"All right. First, touch the one above you to the left that looks like a backwards 'P' with waves around it. Then touch the one below it that looks like a waning crescent moon, but don't remove your finger. You have to keep pressing that one while you reach for the final one. It's above you on the right and looks like a big 'O' with lines in the middle."

Devin took a moment to locate each symbol, then reached out, touching each one as Gage had instructed. At the sound of the cell doors unlatching, she spun around and came face to face with her maker.

* * * * *

Aryiah stiffened and pulled her hands from Damarius'. The electric current running through her veins and the sudden awareness flooding her mind had her racing for the door. "Devin is here!"

She didn't need to turn to know Damarius was hot on her heels as they fled his room. "What? Aryiah, wait!"

Waiting wasn't an option. Aryiah ran down the hallway, trying to understand why Devin would be in Ovialell, let alone in the goddess' castle. At first, she thought maybe Devin too had been triggered to become a Witch, but the thought left her just as quickly as it had come, as she was struck with the knowledge that broke her heart.

With Aradia's omnipotent magick flowing through her, Aryiah knew something terrible had happened. Devin was now a vampire. And if that wasn't devastating enough, things were about to get much, much worse.

As they reached the stairs which led to the dungeon, Damarius caught up with Aryiah, grabbing her arm. "Tell me what's going on," he demanded.

Aryiah gazed into her mate's concerned eyes and shared what she knew with him via their mind bond.

The deep creases that pulled at his brow were enough to communicate he understood the severity of the situation.

Gage is in the dungeon. He is obviously the reason Devin's here. Aryiah . . . he's her Sire.

Damarius' words hit Aryiah like a punch to the gut delivered by a prize fighter. She knew Gage was in the dungeon, and they had talked about how he had special powers that other vampires didn't, but this—changing her best friend into a creature of death and destruction—this was the last straw. She was going to end him, right now.

As Aradia's memories flooded her mind, Aryiah knew exactly how to banish Gage. With a hard set to her jaw, she prepared the spell in her head as they descended the stairs. But as soon as she rounded the corner, Aryiah was brought up short by the sight of Devin embracing Gage outside the iron cell.

Aryiah stood frozen in a state of denial as she stared at her best friend wrapped in the arms of the man who'd been sent to kill her. Her chest constricted as she was struck with Devin's emotions and reality set in. Devin was reveling in being a vampire . . . she actually *liked* it.

The spark of light that Devin always seemed to carry within her was gone, replaced by a dark, twisted desire to lose herself in this new life. Aryiah felt a tear run down her cheek as Devin smiled at her over Gage's shoulder—a smile full of fangs and menace.

Aryiah's emotions and resulting hesitation cost them the element of surprise. In the blink of an eye, Gage pushed Devin behind him, protecting her with his own body. "We'll be back for you, Witch," he said, taunting them before they raced down the hall and out of sight.

Aryiah dropped to her knees as Damarius wrapped his arms around her shoulders. "Aryiah, come on, we can stop them at the portal. Vampires can't shade, and it's their only way off Upper World."

Damarius may have been in a hurry to stop Gage, but the idea of killing or banishing her best friend left Aryiah motionless on the cold dungeon floor.

Damarius gently shook Aryiah again, hoping to jostle her out of her shocked state. But as he looked at her face the shock quickly became his instead.

Tears of thick silver now ran down her cheeks, leaving a glowing trail upon her skin. He shot to his feet and cried, "Goddess, please hurry! I need your help."

The goddess appeared in a flash and quickly took in the scene: Aryiah crying silver tears on the floor, her arms wrapped tight around her middle, the cell door standing wide, the prisoner missing from within, and Damarius pacing as he worked his hand through his hair over and over. "What happened?" Diana asked as she knelt next to Aryiah's shaking form.

"The vampire somehow turned Aryiah's best friend from behind his prison cell. She was apparently drawn here to save her Sire. They just made their escape." He stalked back and forth, itching to shift and go after the vampires, but the thought of leaving his mate in this torn state was something he could never do.

The goddess placed one hand on Aryiah's forehead and the other on her heart. After several excruciating seconds, she gently guided Aryiah to lay on the floor, then rose to face Damarius. "Aradia's power is leaking out through Aryiah's emotions. I've put her in a light magickal coma until she can level out the two parts of her soul. Aryiah needs to learn how to control Aradia's magic, because right now, her emotions are getting in the way."

Damarius' anger flared as he stared at his beautiful mate now lying on the cold stone floor.

"Please take her to my room. I'll be there once I've stopped the vampires." The abrupt tone of his voice couldn't compare to the violence he was getting ready to unleash on Gage and his now-accomplice, Devin. As he began to shift into his wolf, he heard his goddess' voice once more.

"I'll take care of Aryiah, but you need to be mindful of your actions and do the same."

The feel of the cold concrete on his paws matched the cold feeling the goddess' words caused within. He knew exactly what she meant. Aryiah had just lost her best friend, and if he were to kill Devin now—before Aryiah had a chance to process everything—he'd run the risk of losing *her* as well.

He shook the thought from his head and shaded directly to the portal, on high alert as he waited for the vamps to show themselves. Within seconds, Damarius caught sight of movement in the trees. Scanning the forest, he looked between the thick evergreen trunks, trying to pinpoint the location of the approaching threat. Suddenly, a flash of color drew his eyes to the skyline. A streak of red raced from one tree-top to the next. Damarius tracked Devin through the branches, and wasn't surprised when she and Gage landed directly in front of him.

The three began their predatory dance. Stalking each other while constantly shifting their positions in an effort to gauge which of them would make the first move. Damarius angled himself in front of the portal in an effort to block their exit.

"One wolf? You think you alone can stop us?" Gage mocked.

The low growl that resonated from Damarius' chest was the only warning he gave before launching himself directly at Gage. He may be only one wolf, but he was the Leader of the Wild Hunt, and that gave him a few special abilities Gage was fortunately unaware of.

Before the vampire could pivot out of his way, Damarius summoned the magick he used on the hunt, becoming nothing more than a ghostly apparition of his wolf form, twice his normal size.

The shocked expression on Gage's face was satisfying as Damarius sank his phantom teeth into the vampire's upper thigh, but even more satisfying was the scream that tore from Gage's throat. "Impossible!"

Damarius and his wolves were the only ones with this ability. This misted, yet solid form was the state they took when racing in the night sky beside the goddess on every full moon.

Riding the lunar beams in their non-corporeal state while ensnaring their prey was a high they all looked forward to each month. Being their leader afforded Damarius with yet another special privilege—calling on his phantom state any time he needed.

The satisfaction of having Gage in his clutches sent a shot of adrenaline racing through his veins. The blows the vampire was pounding into his back had no effect as Damarius dug in and yanked him to the ground. Just as he was about to open his jaw and go for the vampire's throat, he heard Gage shout, "Run, Devin! Go back through the portal and return to my home. The Darkling will be in touch."

At Gage's words, Damarius froze. Seeing Devin's panicked expression out of the corner of his eye left him torn between ending the fight with his current prey, or stopping Aryiah's best friend from escaping and making contact with this *Darkling*. His mind was made up when he watched Devin's muscles tense as she prepared to make her escape.

Damarius lifted his head from Gage's leg and flew towards Devin's back. Sadly, the only thing his teeth snagged on was the hem of her leather pants as she disappeared through the silver liquid of the portal.

He came to an abrupt stop, his nose only inches from the glowing exit, then spun around to face Gage once more. Damarius maintained his position in front of the portal, the anger of losing his prey causing his ghostly form to expand and retract with heavy breaths.

His keen eyes darted to the wound on the vampire's leg. It was already starting to heal. Damarius knew Gage would be up and ready to fight again within seconds.

He quickly weighed the idea of going after Devin. But in order to use the portal or shade to Obsidian to begin his search, he'd first have to shift back into his solid form, and that would take time and energy he simply couldn't spare.

"Face it, wolf. You've lost. Devin is mine, and together we will end you and your soon to be Witch."

With Gage's words stinging his ears, Damarius launched himself through the air once more. Gage must have realized fighting him in this state was a waste of effort, because he quickly maneuvered around Damarius' incoming attack and dove through the portal without a backward glance.

As his ethereal paws touched solid ground, Damarius shifted back to his human form. The choice between tracking Gage and Devin or checking on Aryiah tugged at his brain, but it only took seconds for his heart to make up his mind.

CHAPTER THIRTY-FOUR

Damarius immediately shaded to his bedroom and found Aryiah wrapped in the blankets on his massive bed. The sight of her tiny frame lost within the yards of material had him racing to her side, as if drowning in the luxurious fabric was another threat he needed to protect her from.

"Aryiah, can you hear me?"

The light breeze that swept across his back announced his goddess' arrival. "Yes, she can hear you, Damarius. Talk to her. For I believe only you will be able to set her mind at ease."

The gentle touch of Diana's hand on his shoulder reminded him that he too had some news to share. Turning to face her, he gestured towards the door with a nod of his head. Once in the hall, Damarius relayed what had happened with the vampires and watched as Diana's face fell at his mention of the Darklings.

"So I was right. The Darklings have returned and are using

their magick to enhance the vampires in their fight against us."

"Yes, my lady. That does seem to be the case. Do you wish me to track them now? I'm confident it won't take long to locate them."

Diana hesitated, causing him to stiffen while he awaited her response. He was ready to find and kill Gage for what he did to Devin, and by their association, to Aryiah. But again, the thought of leaving his mate had his heart flinching with a twinge of pain.

"No, Damarius. It's Aryiah who needs you now, and to be honest . . . we need her. No one knows of Aradia's return, so training her to control her magick is now our top priority." With a confident smile she continued, "Let them think they've escaped to continue their plans, for when they learn of *our* plans . . . it will be too late for them to react with anything but fear."

Damarius breathed a sigh of relief as he bowed to the goddess. "Thank you, my lady. I just pray our connection is strong enough for me to reach Aryiah in her comatose state."

"Don't doubt your bond, Damarius. Aryiah loves you, and those feelings will be what pulls her free of her emotional struggles."

The goddess dissipated in a swirl of silver smoke as her words wrapped around his heart. *Aryiah loves you . . .*

Even though she'd seemed to accept their mated bond, Aryiah hadn't yet said the words. Damarius approached his bed once more, hoping the goddess was right.

He took a seat next to his mate, reached for her hand, and struggled with what to say. He closed his eyes and found comfort in the motion of his thumb tracing tiny circles over the back of her smooth hand. Releasing his fears, he finally let the words simply spill from his lips. "Aryiah, I love you. I know you're struggling, but please come back to me. We can face anything together, but without you . . . I don't think I can go on."

As the words hit his ears, he rolled his eyes. They sounded so damn cliché, but they couldn't have been truer. He had no idea how he'd be able to go on fulfilling his duties of protecting the goddess, leading the wolves, and training the Witches without her. He lived thousands of years without one distraction, but could now only focus on his demise if he were to lose his mate.

A slight buzzing sensation penetrated his mind which put a stop to his downward spiral. He reached up, brushing the hair off Aryiah's forehead, and gently traced a line down her cheek with the back of his fingers. He leaned in and placed a kiss in the wake of his touch. Her cheek was warm, and he found himself unable to pull away. He pressed his lips a little more firmly into the hollow of her cheek and closed his eyes.

"Please, baby. Wake up for me."

A small twitch of Aryiah's hand snapped his head up and his eyes open. The positive sign was like a shot of heroin through his veins, causing his heart to race and his mind to spin. He immediately retraced his actions, trying to pinpoint exactly what he did to elicit her response. *I touched her cheek, then spoke into her mind.* Hoping the latter was the key to her recovery, he tried it again.

"Aryiah, squeeze my hand if you can hear me."

To his crushing disappointment, the only response to his mental communication was a slight humming inside his head. He immediately tried his second option, running a finger down her cheek, this time expanding his stoke to include the side of her arm. His heart leapt when Aryiah's hand flinched again, tightening ever so slightly inside of his. A sense of hope flooded his chest. He took a deep breath and continued to run his hand up and down her arm, the motion probably more reassuring to him than her.

With excitement fueling him, he continued to rub her arm, switching from one to the other, then moved to her face, placing gentle strokes across her cheeks and brow. But after a short time, his tender care was still only resulting in a small twitch of her hand.

With his head sagging and hopes crushed, he tried speaking into her mind once more. *"Please, Aryiah, if you can hear me, tell me what I must do."*

The buzzing in his head had him suddenly berating himself. *Dammit, why didn't I realize this before?*

It was obvious to him now . . . Aryiah was the source of the noise in his head. She was trying to respond to him through their bonded link.

"Baby, can you hear me?" he thought, putting his theory to the test.

The slight tingle in his brain had him celebrating. Even if it was a tiny victory, it was one more step to breaking her out of this frozen state.

Unable to control his excitement, he leaned down and placed a kiss on Aryiah's still lips. Her hand tightened around his and the buzzing in his head grew to a dull roar. A smile spread across his face. He leaned in and increased the passion of their connection, pressing his lips a little more firmly to hers, and wound his hand through the tangles of her hair.

Her response was immediate.

Aryiah's entire arm flinched and the noise in his head sounded as if a swarm of bees had somehow permeated his mind. With excitement and desperation motivating him, he angled his body closer to hers.

Lying with his chest pressed to her side, he could feel the increased depth of her breathing and took it as a good sign. *"Aryiah, I think the key to releasing you is to stimulate your senses. Bear with me, my love, as I use our intimate connection to pull you back to me."*

With a steady hum in his head and tiny movements breaking out all over Aryiah's body, he was confident he was on the right track. Leaning forward, he kissed her again, lingering just as before. Freeing his fingers from her hair, he felt her breath hitch when he rubbed down the side of her neck, slowing continuing down passed her breasts.

A few moments of kissing and caressing was all he needed to know that his plan was going to work. Her movements had increased and he was starting to hear actual words breaking through the white noise in his head. Words like *"yes,"* and *"more."*

Excited his touch alone was all it would take to bring Aryiah back to him, he followed her silent instruction, continuing his light caresses. The arch to her back told him that they were almost there. A little more stimulation and she would come back to him fully.

Sliding a hand across her stomach and down her thigh, he made his return pass up the sensitive area of her inner leg, stopping suddenly when Aryiah jolted upright.

CHAPTER THIRTY-FIVE

"Oh, Damarius," Aryiah sobbed, falling into his arms. She snuggled close as he repositioned them to settle into bed. "Thank you," she said, kissing his cheek. "Your touch is what anchors me to this world. I was so angry, frightened, and confused over seeing Devin, that my mind just snapped. With my emotions out of control, Aradia's power overwhelmed me, and I couldn't process either of them . . . my feelings or her magick."

Damarius pulled the silk sheets over them but continued to rub his hand along her back. It felt so reassuring to be in his arms again, that Aryiah almost felt at peace . . . *almost.*

"What are we going to do about Gage and Devin?" she asked.

"The goddess' main priority is you, Aryiah. We need to complete your training and make sure something like this doesn't happen again. You have to be able to control Aradia's magick at all times. Even in a horrible, twisted situation like the one with Devin."

She rose up on her elbow and turned to face him. "What happen to Devin? I mean, *how* did it happen? If Gage was locked up here, how is something like that even possible?"

Damarius smoothed a strand of hair off her shoulder before answering. "I don't know. I assume it's due to one of his enhanced powers. But what I do know is that he plans to use Devin as a way to get to you, and that . . . we cannot allow."

Not wanting to let her mate down, Aryiah jumped up from the bed. "You're right. We need to start my training immediately. Then, with a boost from Aradia, I'll kick his ass and hopefully save Devin in the process."

The look on Damarius' face as she headed for the bathroom left a sinking feeling in her chest. She knew then, there would be no way to save Devin. She was going to have to accept that her friend was truly beyond help.

As Aryiah continued towards the shower she pretended not to see his reaction. She needed some time alone to ease the ache facing that reality had caused. She turned the knobs and let the water run until steam filled the room, then stepped into the enclosure, letting her tears mix with the hot water.

She cried and cried, feeling as if the history between her and Devin was washing down the drain. The person, or thing Devin now was, carried no resemblance to the woman she'd been friends with for the past ten years. That knowledge had slammed into her in the dungeon when she'd been hit full on with Devin's emotions. Devin had been happy about becoming a vampire, and that was something Aryiah would never understand. How could her friend like the idea of killing people and being evil?

She shook her head, unable to process the thought. A surge of frustration was quickly replaced with anger, and Aryiah was suddenly motivated to prepare for their next confrontation. Steeling herself against the cold, she wiped her eyes and exited the shower, walking straight into the bedroom. She found Damarius dressed and waiting patiently by the door with a smile on his face.

Holding out his hand he said, "I figured you'd like to go back to your apartment and gather some things, like your clothes and important belongings, before we begin your training."

She smiled at the fact that he must have read her mind and simply replied, "Yes, that would be great."

With a swipe of his hand, Damarius clothed her, then wrapped her in his embrace once more. Together, they shaded to her apartment and began to gather her things. It didn't take long to sort through her clothes and throw the chosen items into her suitcase. Next, they headed to the living room, where she started sifting through all her books and pictures.

"What will happen when I complete my rites? I mean, technically I'll be dead, so will people be fed some story and hold a funeral for me or what?"

With a solemn tone Damarius answered, "No, my love. Once you wake as a citizen of Ovialell, everyone who had contact with you in the human world will lose all their memories of you. In their eyes, you won't have died, but will simply cease to exist in the folds of history in the first place."

Aryiah dropped the photo album that was currently in her hand. "You mean Rochelle and my ex-husband won't remember me at all? Not even my own mother?"

"No, Aryiah. No one will remember you. You will be wiped from human history so that you can live your eternal life free to move about the realms as the goddess you truly are."

His words stung, but she was happy he didn't try to sugar coat it for her. She gathered her strength, which she now recognized as a spark from Aradia, picked up the picture album, and gently placed it on the coffee table. Taking one last look around her apartment, she sighed and said her mental goodbye to the only life she'd ever known.

After narrowly escaping Damarius' grasp, Devin came flying out the other side of the portal, landing back in the center of Obsidian with a hard thump. In a flurry of motion that left leaves whirling in the streets, Devin then sped back to Gage's apartment. Much to her relief, Gage joined her shortly after.

"Oh thank god you escaped." Devin flew into his arms, not thinking twice about wrapping herself around him. She began kissing and licking her way around his neck as her fangs extended.

"Wait," came his sharp command.

"Why?" Devin asked as she continued to rub herself against him.

He grabbed her shoulders and forced her to look at him, staring deep into her eyes. "Because your Sire commanded you to." His tone was full of menace and impatience.

She wiggled out of his grip and walked towards the

mattress on the floor. Lowering herself down to the bed, she stretched out to give him a nice view of her ass. "Color me confused, but I thought we were past the small talk. I mean, you did fuck me and turn me into a vampire already."

"Yes, I did. And that was a mistake." He turned his back to her and walked into the small kitchen. She watched as he began pulling out strange bottles filled with small white shards that looked like tiny bones.

She flew off the bed and moved to stand beside the counter, pretending to watch him work, but really . . . she just wanted to be close to him. "Why would you say that? Changing me was not a mistake, and I'm sure you don't regret what happened between us in that dungeon." She licked her fangs, trying to add to her taunt.

He slammed down a glass container, shattering it on the hard stone. "I never wanted to be a Sire! And for me . . . I have no idea what it means to have made a vampire while in the dreamscape."

Devin digested his unsure tone and hoped that he was just nervous about being a new Sire and not really planning to reject her. Deciding to give him some time, she quickly changed the subject.

"What are you doing? What are those?"

"I'm preparing to summon the Darkling who bestowed me with my powers."

He emptied the last bottle of white shards onto the

164

counter and began moving them around, guiding them into specific places. After watching him position the tiny objects, Devin realized that she was staring at the shape of a skeletal hand.

"Stand in the corner until I call you forward, and Devin . . . don't defy me in front of him." His voice carried a dangerous edge to it that had her suddenly wanting to obey his every command.

Slinking to the corner, Devin watched as Gage placed his hand over the tiny bones, pressing down on them until Devin smelled the scent of blood. Suddenly, even though there were no lights on in the apartment, it seemed to get darker and an eerie shape began to coalesce in the middle of the room.

Devin watched as a robed figure began to take shape, then held her breath when it raised its head, piercing her with a pair of iridescent white eyes. It looked human . . . mostly. But it moved with a strange gait, lumbering like whatever was hidden within the folds of its cloak made it hard to walk.

"You summoned me?" The creepy voice sounded like razors on a chalkboard to Devin's ears.

"Yes. I've sired a vampire and need to know the consequences of the action, since the situation was . . . unique." Gage got straight to the point, which pleased Devin, because the idea of lingering in this being's presence any longer than necessary sent chills up her spine.

The Darkling hobbled towards Gage, then in an action

that struck Devin as strange, he reached out with his hand and gently stroked the white shards lying on the counter.

"What is so unique about a vampire siring another?"

Gage shifted on his feet, which had Devin wondering if he was nervous about sharing the intimate details of her making, or if he too simply didn't feel comfortable in the Darkling's presence.

"I used one of the powers you bestowed upon me to summon her into the dreamscape, and while mating with her, I drank her dry. She woke back in the human realm, but within a day, completed the transition and arrived in Ovialell a full vampire."

With his back to her, the Darkling raised his cloaked head and Devin noticed Gage's stoic expression flinched slightly under the scrutiny of the creature's gaze.

"You are free to use your powers as you wish, but since my dark magick flows through you, all that you do is also bound by that connection. Your vampires will not gain your power, but the bond you share will be very unique."

What the fuck does that mean? Devin thought, as she watched Gage nod his head. Her keen eyesight then caught the bob of his Adam's apple as he swallowed hard. "What if I were to choose her as my mate?"

Devin sucked in a shocked breath then regretted the action when the Darkling turned, leveling her with his eerie gaze. "Any vampire you create will be . . . tainted." He cocked his head as if popping his neck in and out of place as he crept in her direction. "They will have a tendency to become more vicious than those created by regular vampires. If she can handle the increased darkness that will always be a part of her," he stopped within arm's reach, "then you've made a wise choice."

The Darkling's right hand suddenly shot out, grabbing her entire face in his grip. Devin's body was rendered immobile while her mind was flooded with images. Scenes of herself ripping throats open with her fangs, fighting with the speed and strength of a true supernatural being. But the image that had her core pulsing was one of she and Gage having sex while soaked in their enemies' blood.

Released from the Darkling's grip, Devin's eyes rolled back in her head as she stumbled backwards. She used the wall behind her to steady herself, quickly regaining her bearings.

His scratchy voice and demented smile sent chills over her skin as he said, "You've chosen well. She will be a great asset to our cause." Turning to Gage he continued. "Enjoy your new mate."

He then began to disintegrate, collapsing into an oily black ball of matter. The last thing Devin noticed before he completely disappeared was his left arm protruding from under his cloak, a left arm that ended in a handless nub.

* * * * *

A sense of relief settled over Gage now that the Darkling was gone. He prided himself on being the one vampire who'd been chosen to receive their dark magick, but he'd never be so foolish as to think they were on equal ground. When the creature had grabbed Devin by the face, his protective instinct flared to life, but as he tried to move to defend his progeny, he found himself frozen in place.

"Do you feel better about turning me now?" Devin's sensual voice pulled him out of his revere. As he looked across his room at her, he remembered the Darkling's last words. *"Enjoy your new mate."*

He took a deep breath and stalked towards her, refusing to use his enhanced speed. He wanted to take his time and get to know her, and yes, he planned to enjoy every minute of it.

As they met in the middle of the room, their frenzied kisses quickly turned into shredded clothes. The feel of her body under his hands was like a heaven he'd long forgotten.

"Gage, did you mean it when you said you wanted me as your mate?" He could sense the fear of disappointment that lingered under the surface of her voice.

With his hand around her throat he lifted his head from the silken flesh of her shoulder and looked straight into her eyes. "I never intended to become a Sire, but when we were together in the dreamscape you invaded my mind, and I lost control. I regretted it at first, and you were right, I was pissed off that it happened at all. But then remembering the sexual thoughts that flooded your mind and catching a glimpse of your dark side, I started thinking it might not be so bad after all."

"Wow, you really know how to make a girl feel special." She bared her teeth, causing him to smile.

"You wanted answers and those are mine. Take it for what it is. Be my mate and fight by my side, or not. Either way, you are still mine." He knew his tone was harsh, but he wasn't ready to admit that he thought about being with her after their initial encounter. Actually, he wasn't even ready to admit it to himself, since it had taken him completely by surprise at the time.

With a feral look in her eyes, Devin pried his hand from her throat, ripped off their remaining clothes, and threw him onto the mattress. She straddled him, her long red hair flowing forward over her shoulders.

"I'll be your mate and fight by your side, but you're right . . . I did have a dark side before you turned me, and most of it had to do with my sexual appetite, so I hope you're ready to feed me."

She struck so fast he didn't have time to respond. Her fangs were buried in the thick flesh of his left pec as she moved atop him.

Lifting her head, blood dripped from her fangs and onto her chest, creating the most erotic picture. Gage raised his head and placed his tongue just right to catch a drop in his mouth.

With a growl, Devin flew across the room and stood naked in his kitchen. "Come here."

Gage wasn't used to being told what to do, but having her order him to come service her was an order he was willing to take. Following her instruction, he joined her in the kitchen, pushing aside the glass and bones from the large island. Growls and moans filled the room as they began to explore each other, then Devin again flew from his grasp and began rummaging through the kitchen drawers. A mix of depraved curiosity and a shred of fear shot through him as he watched her pull out a thin metal ring and a lighter.

"Now it's time to have some fun."

CHAPTER THIRTY-SEVEN

Damarius watched as Aryiah summoned her fifth energy ball out of thin air. Her training was going unbelievably well, and the things she'd accomplished were far superior to any other Witch he'd ever trained.

"In your apartment you had to recite a spell to summon an energy ball. What's changed that you don't need to do so now?" His question was meant for them both. He truly did want to know the answer, but by asking for her response, he hoped she'd gain an understanding to the power she now wielded.

"I'm not sure I can explain it. I feel like Aradia's magick is located in a pool deep inside of me, and whenever I want to create something or do something, I simply think about it and then dip into that pool of magick . . . then it just happens."

Aryiah's response made sense. Before they began her training, which started with intense meditation sessions, her magick could have easily overflowed from its *'pool'* and flooded her entire being, which could explain what happened in the dungeon.

"Actually, I think you explained it perfectly." Damarius smiled proudly as he approached his beautiful mate. "I believe your training is almost complete. I just have one final test."

"What's that?" she asked with a cocky tilt to her head.

"I want you to transform into your wolf."

The color drained from Aryiah's face and her eyes grew to twice their normal size. "You want me to purposely turn into a wolf?"

"Yes. You did it before when your body and magick were in a state of heightened sensitivity, so we both know it's possible. But what we need is for you to be able to call upon it at will."

Damarius stood firm with his arms crossed over his broad chest while he waited for Aryiah's response. He could sense her emotions spiking, teetering between fear and doubt, and excitement and confidence.

With a firm set to her jaw, Aryiah took three steps back and closed her eyes. Damarius watched as a green shimmer of magick ran over her skin, then stood awe-struck once more as he stared at her, now a gorgeous silver wolf with piercing blue eyes.

Aryiah gently padded forward and rubbed her head against his leg. He ran his hand through her fur, digging in with his fingers to feel her soft undercoat.

"I knew you could do it. Now, would you like to go for a run?"

She pranced in place, her excitement the positive response he was hoping for. He quickly joined her in wolf form, and the next thing he heard was Aryiah's voice inside his head.

This is amazing! Everything is just so . . . heightened.

It only took a moment for Damarius to realize they could still use their mated bond to share thoughts, but only while they both held the same form, or unless they were on a shamanic journey. *"Just wait until we get outside."*

Damarius led Aryiah out the open side door of the training room. He watched as she took in her surroundings and was thrilled at the jubilant emotions he could feel radiating from her.

He could have sworn she flashed him a wolfish smile right before racing into the surrounding forest. He flexed his powerful legs and sprinted after her.

They spent hours running through the trees, playing and hunting until they reached the northern shore of Dalestri.

Aryiah laid down on the white sandy beach, and Damarius joined her after a quick security scan of the surrounding area.

"What's that island out there?" she asked.

"Themiscyra is home of the Amazons. Their leader, Kylie, has always been a friend and ally to the goddess."

"Amazons. As in large beautiful warrior women?" The hint of

jealousy layering the thought had Damarius stifling a laugh.

"Yes. Their increased size and magickally enhanced skills make them the perfect warriors. But as for beautiful . . . no one compares to you."

Aryiah's wolfish grin returned right before the magick shimmered over her silver fur, transforming her back into her beautiful self. Damarius followed her lead and within seconds they were lying on the beach in each other's arms.

"Well, I'll be the judge of that when you take me to their island and introduce me." Sinking her toes into the pure white sand, Aryiah looked up at the lavender tinted sky. Even though the sun was shining bright gold, there always seemed to be a silver haze that hung in the air. "This world never ceases to amaze me," Aryiah said. "What causes the sky to look like that?"

"Do you mean the silver glow?"

"Yes. It seems to surround everything."

"It's because Upper World is home to the Goddess Diana. Her magick comes from the spirit realm, which gives off a silver hue. This world is coated in her magick."

Aryiah sighed. "Everything is just so beautiful here."

Damarius felt his chest tighten and thought about holding back his next words, but as he recalled his confrontation with Gage and Devin, he knew they needed to be said. "Yes, but you can never let your guard down, Aryiah. Aradia's return is proof enough that dangerous times lie ahead."

Aryiah's smile collapsed as she rolled onto her back, displacing the sand. "I know."

* * * * *

Damarius' words tugged her emotions tighter than a stretched violin string. One pluck and she was bound to snap. She knew her plans to visit the Amazons, or simply enjoying the company of her sexy lover on the shores of Dalestri, were all things that were going to have to wait. She needed to focus on controlling and developing her magick so when she took her place with the Witches, she wouldn't let them, her mother, or the citizens of Ovialell down. The goddess had explained that until Aryiah completed her rites, which would complete their coven, their collective strength would remain diminished.

Aryiah closed her eyes, picturing Devin's fanged smile peering at her from over Gage's shoulder. She could now level the emotions the image caused, but unfortunately still couldn't soften the pain the blow inflicted to her heart. Devin was lost and Aryiah could only imagine the plans Gage had for the two of them. She was sure the Witches would need to be at their full strength for whatever was coming next.

Suddenly overwhelmed with the urge to complete her rites, Aryiah jumped up from the sand, holding her hand out to Damarius. Once he placed his hand in hers, she yanked him into the Shadowlands, shading them both into the goddess' upper throne room.

The loving smile and tilt of his head relayed he understood what she was thinking. She squeezed his hand and called out, "Mother, are you here?"

Diana's appearance was instantaneous. "Hearing your call lifts my heart. What can I do for you, Daughter?"

"I want to complete my rites as soon as possible. I have my magick under control and the urgent feeling I have is something I can't ignore."

With a knowing smile on her face, the goddess responded. "I've been thinking the same thing. Winter Solstice isn't for another two months, but Samhain is only three days away." As Diana approached them both, Aryiah stared at the faint silver glow surrounding the goddess. "The Witches' New Year is the perfect time for you to take your rightful place. I'll start the preparations immediately."

After *"getting to know each other,"* Gage took Devin through the streets of Obsidian, showing her his favorite haunts and explaining how everything worked in their world. After being approached by an old flame, the exchange of some heated words and a few splatters of blood, Devin quickly established that he was hers. Gage watched the confrontation with a smirk on his face and couldn't be happier that he'd chosen this fierce woman as his mate.

As they walked out of the bar, Devin looked around and continued as if nothing had happened. "Obsidian is beautiful, and the fact that it's always dark, except for the blood moons' glow is really something."

"Yes. The goddess is gracious in acknowledging the needs of all citizens of Ovialell."

Devin stopped, dropping her gaze from the red-tinted sky. "Then why are you siding with the Darkling to fight against her?"

The question struck him as odd, considering that her bloodlust was even more intense than his own. "Just because the goddess accepts us as citizens of Ovialell doesn't mean that she accepts our ways or looks upon us as anything more than lower level beings. We share Lower World with the demons of Hel, the worst creatures of us all. So when the Darkling approached me, promising a rise in class for vampires and demons alike if we fought with him, I jumped at the opportunity. If you haven't noticed, no one in the vampire community is special . . . except me."

"I get that. And I love that you are completely unique, but how does fighting the goddess guarantee a rise in class for vampires or demons?"

"The Darkling will overthrow Diana and her precious Witches, taking over all of Ovialell. I'm sure during your *visit* you realized that vampires aren't usually permitted in Upper World. The only reason you were able to reach it through the portal was because you were being drawn to my side after your initial change. But traditionally, we are held to Obsidian, and are only able to use the portal to travel to the human world for our food. If we were able to travel freely, we could access all the realms and . . . " His words trailed off. Suddenly worried he shouldn't be sharing this information without the Darkling's permission, he quickly changed the subject.

"What we need to be worrying about is if we'll be able to

get back into Upper World a second time. I think my magick will allow us access, but it's something that we need to test soon, because killing your friend before she completes her rites is still our number one priority."

A look of feral anticipation fell over Devin's features, pleasing him that she was still willing to destroy her best friend. When they had discussed it earlier, Devin shared her feelings about Aryiah and how she'd always felt second best in their human lives. Gage took advantage of her personal memory and used his dark magick to turn Devin's small insecurity into a full-fledge hatred. Now, full of dark magick and bloodlust, Devin's tiniest spark of resentment had been replaced with a deadly, all-consuming vengeance.

"Let's do this," Devin replied.

* * * * *

Devin and Gage sat on the stone bench in front of the floating portal as they waited for the sun to set on the rest of Ovialell.

"Let's go over the plan again," Devin demanded.

"If I make it through the portal, I'll come right back to get you. It shouldn't take more than five seconds. Once there, we'll use the trees to reach the castle, then use the same door you used before to begin our search for Aryiah within," Gage explained.

"Why can't you just call her to you in the dreamscape like you did me?"

"My dream-walking only works on humans. Plus, from the beginning, Aryiah seemed to be immune to my skills."

Devin grabbed his head and thrust her tongue into his mouth, kissing him hard and quick. "Well, once we find her, you won't need any special skills to kill her, because that pleasure will be all mine."

She looked up at the large building directly across from where they sat. The large clock set into the stone reminded her of Big Ben. It showed the accurate times for each of the levels of Ovialell. It had just turned 8 p.m. in Upper World.

She stood next to the portal and kissed Gage again before he stepped through. Within seconds his arm appeared through the shimmering silver and pulled her forward. They stepped through together, recognizing the flame-lit path that stretched out in front of them.

"I knew it would work," Gage said, with a cocky smirk on his face.

"Then let's go. I want my fangs buried in her neck within the hour," Devin replied.

They flew into the trees and raced towards the castle unimpeded. But before reaching the edge of the forest, Gage stopped and gestured for her to do the same. He motioned to the path that was a mere ten feet away from where Damarius and Aryiah were currently strolling hand in hand.

After leaving the goddess' throne room, Aryiah and Damarius decided to continue their exploration of Dalestri.

As they walked along a cobblestone path, Aryiah was mesmerized by tall evergreens and the beautiful torches that radiated an ethereal blue-green flame. "Where are we going?"

"I want to show you the castle's portal. It's the only way off Upper World for those who live in the area but are unable to shade."

They continued down the path, talking about the citizens and the layout of Dalestri and its surrounding villages when Aryiah suddenly felt a sense of warning.

"Someone's watching us," she sent into Damarius' mind.

The feel of his hand tightening in hers indicated he was on high alert. *"Yes, I know. Just continue to walk and talk out loud as if we're none the wiser,"* he sent in response.

Suddenly, Devin and Gage dropped from the trees, landing directly in their path.

Damarius pushed her behind him, his broad back shielding her against the threat. Peering over his shoulder, Aryiah saw Devin crouched in all black attire. It was a look she wasn't used to, but it was Devin's bared fangs that threatened Aryiah's control.

"Why are you doing this?" Aryiah pleaded.

"Because I can't tell you how sick I am of hearing how different and special you think you are. With the 'odd' things that always seemed to happen to you, and how blessed you felt when you got that great job at such a young age. You spent your life alone, acting like a martyr after your father died, refusing to live life with the money he'd left you. Stupid! You always thought you were better than me. Well guess what . . . now I'm as special as you, and you're going to pay for making me feel second best."

The crushing words had Aryiah trembling and grabbing Damarius for support.

"Hold it together, my love. She is no longer the person you once knew. These words are not her own."

Damarius' statement penetrated her mind as she dropped her head, resting it between his shoulder blades. She knew he was right; Devin was truly lost to her, but the idea of fighting and likely killing her best friend crashed over her in a wave of sadness. Aryiah only had seconds to wallow before Damarius' warned, *"Prepare yourself, they're about to attack."*

Gathering her strength, she lifted her head and a sense of peace and power radiated throughout her entire body. She stepped around Damarius, positioning herself in front of him. "I'm so sorry you ever felt that way, and even more sorry to have lost you to him," she gestured to Gage, "but I will not stand here and let you try to hurt me or my mate."

Devin lunged forward, fangs bared, but suddenly Gage held out an arm to stop her. "Not yet, my dear. There's something you don't know about the wolf."

To Aryiah's surprise, Gage revealed Damarius' secret to them all.

"You can't hurt him in his phantom form, but he can latch on and devour you with his teeth," the vampire finished.

"That would have been nice to know," Aryiah thought, feeling slighted about being left in the dark.

"I'm sorry, my love. After you woke from your coma, everything happened so fast, I simply forgot to tell you. But get ready, because you're about to see it firsthand."

Damarius didn't bother with any posturing or monologue, he simply shifted into his wolf then faded to his ghostly form. Aryiah, Devin, and Gage stood shell-shocked for a moment, all looking at the enormous ethereal wolf. Then in a frenzy of sudden movements and one loud shout, Damarius had Devin on the ground, his teeth buried in her neck.

Aryiah stood stunned, while fury blossomed on Gage's

face. She turn to run, but using his vampire speed, he landed behind her before she could move. Holding her tightly by the arms, he positioned his fangs near her throat. "You kill my mate, and I'll kill yours," Gage yelled at Damarius.

Aryiah watched Damarius remove his teeth from Devin's neck. Her friend didn't waste any time scooting away from the giant spirit wolf, one hand clawing at the ground while the other still held her bleeding throat.

"That's right, wolf. We may not be able to kill you, but we can certainly kill her. And as long as I keep killing your triggered Witches, you and your goddess will never be strong enough to stop us."

Aryiah stared into Damarius eyes, hoping he could still sense what she was feeling even though they weren't in the same form. She needed for him to not react, because Gage's talking had given her time to regain her steely control once more, and she was preparing to give the vampire the shock of his life.

She dipped into the pool of Aradia's magic, closed her eyes, and let the power flow. The silver glow that surrounded them both had Gage screaming out in pain. Within seconds, his hands drifted through her now phantom arms.

Aryiah didn't turn into a wolf, but instead, simply melted against his chest, entering his body in her ghostly form.

Gage's screams filled the forest as silver rays of magick burst from within his body. It looked as if he was being lit up from the inside by a magickal sun, as gold and silver rays streamed out of every single pore. The light show lasted for only a few seconds before Aryiah solidified back into her body while Gage was nothing more than ash on the wind.

* * * * *

Damarius shifted back into his human form and watched Aryiah—now back in her solid state—open her eyes, revealing silver glowing pools which she trained straight on Devin.

"Leave this place and never return." Aryiah's words were amplified with power. The stunned expression on Devin's face and the rapid rise and fall of her chest, revealed just how scared Devin was.

Smart girl, Damarius thought.

Damarius' eyes never left Devin's shocked face, as she scrambled to her feet and immediately fled the scene. "Why did you let her go? She threatened to kill you," he asked Aryiah.

As her eyes returned to normal, Aryiah smiled. "You know I had to. She may have threatened to kill me, but with Aradia's magick coursing through my veins, no one can stand against me. She's simply not a threat. Especially without Gage fueling her rage."

Aryiah grabbed his hand and they began their stroll back towards the castle as if nothing had interrupted them at all.

She kissed his lips, her magick leaving a slight tingling

residue. "How did you know you'd be able to take phantom form?" he asked.

"When Gage was explaining your ability, I realized that as a Witch, I too will run with the Wild Hunt. But since Aradia was the creator of the wolves, I didn't need to transform into my wolf first. I could simply embrace the goddess I used to be and join the ether whenever I want."

Her answer was so simple, like a brush off the cuff, but the abilities she now possessed truly made her unstoppable. Besides her mother, Diana, she was simply the most divine person Damarius had ever known.

"I have one other question for you." He took a deep breath and continued before she had a chance to respond. "Will you marry me?"

Three days later, Aryiah paced in her mother's private quarters as sunlight filtered in through the vertical windows of the tower.

"Will the kiss of death hurt or disrupt my magick in any way?"

"No, my dear. You are already so powerful that I'm not even sure it's necessary, but since you still retain a connection to the human world, I feel like it's better to complete the ritual as usual. Upon waking, you will truly be a citizen of Ovialell and can take your rightful place at my side."

Aryiah sighed deeply. *My rightful place.*

While she was confident in her magick, Aryiah was still unsure about the ceremony her mother had planned for later tonight. With the weight of her new position sitting heavily upon her shoulders, the idea of announcing Aradia's return to all of Ovialell caused a lump to form in her throat.

As she turned and caught sight of herself in the mirror, Aryiah's nerves got the best of her. She could barely believe she'd agreed to marry Damarius on the same night as her initiation rites.

"Are you sure this looks all right?" She twirled in front of the mirror, holding out the gauzy white sections of her wedding dress.

"There has never been a more beautiful goddess," Diana replied.

"Maybe we should postpone the wedding to see how the citizens react to my return first, instead of hitting them with two major announcements at once." She knew her statement was rooted in fear, and her mother must have thought so too, because as the goddess reached for her long raven hair, she smiled a knowing smile.

"Do not fret, my child. You will be loved by all. Some may doubt, but once you hold my book in your hands, you will be welcomed with open arms, for all know that only I and Aradia can command the magick within it."

Once her mother finished braiding her hair and pinning it with a silver, diamond-encrusted crescent moon clip, she turned and wrapped her in a hug.

"Thank you for believing in me," Aryiah whispered.

The two stood embracing as the rest of the Witches filtered into the room.

Aryiah took in the faces of the other Witches, as Diana led

her to the dais in the middle of the floor. "Aryiah, meet your Witches." Gesturing to each of them one by one, the goddess introduced them all. "This is Verta, Fern, Carmen, Camille, Josephina, Lydia, Basha, Dassia, Gayle, Rozalyn, Yuna, and Zaria."

They all bowed to her, already aware of what her position within their ranks would be. Aryiah was to be their queen once more, just as Aradia had been in the past.

Needing to get this done before she lost her nerve, Aryiah laid down on the raised platform, her Witches surrounding her on all sides. As the goddess approached, she closed her eyes and took a deep breath, forcing herself into a deep relaxed state.

There was no spell spoken, just a light kiss from her mother's lips, and then darkness.

Only a few hours must have passed, because upon her waking, Aryiah noticed the waning light filtering throughout the room. She was still surrounded by her Witches, and her mother stood next to her with a beaming smile. "Life must end for life to begin, join us now as daughter and friend."

Once she sat up, they all began cheering and hugging her. She hadn't realized it would be so easy. But this was just the beginning. Next was the actual initiation rite, which was also held in the privacy of her mother's chambers.

As Diana spoke, all the Witches fell to their knees. "Aryiah, you are now a citizen of Ovialell, and your place among the Witches has been chosen. Do you accept the rank of Queen?"

She knew she didn't have a choice; Aradia's powers were far superior to any other Witch here, but to officially accept her place as their queen was truly a monumental step.

Bowing to the goddess, she simply replied, "I accept," and in that moment her magickal life had truly begun. The wind picked up as cheers broke out once again. The goddess now held a gorgeous silver crown encrusted with moonstones and emeralds. After placing it gently on Aryiah's head, all the Witches stood in a circle and linked hands.

As soon as Aryiah completed the connection, a ring of silver magick shot from her heart, racing from Witch to Witch to form an unbreakable circle. Suddenly, the entire group was being lifted into the air as the magickal energy increased in speed.

Everyone closed their eyes and lifted their faces to the crystal dome ceiling. Feeling the moonlight surrounding her, Aryiah closed her eyes and shared in this glorious bonding experience. She could feel each of her sisters in turn, pinpointing each of their specific energies separately. No longer was she alone on this journey, and the unity she felt with these women almost brought her to tears. They were a cohesive unit once again, now that she'd completed their coven of thirteen.

As they eased back down to the ground, she opened her eyes and looked upon them for the first time as her family. She now knew each of their names, and their life experiences since joining the Witches, and they hers in return.

"Thank you for accepting me as your queen once again. While most of you will remember Aradia, I know this may be an adjustment, but please know that I will use all her knowledge and power to be the best queen for you and our people."

After a small celebration of cakes and ale, the Witches left and Aryiah rejoined her mother, who'd been watching from the high-backed wooden chair that sat next to her Book of Shadows.

"Is that what happens every time a new Witch is inducted?" Aryiah asked.

With a light laugh, the goddess answered, "Not exactly. When the coven is complete, the magick does connect them all, but only when the queen is in place do their shared memories flow. It's a way for you to connect to them, and get a sense of their hearts' desire, past and future. That connection will allow you to monitor them at all times."

The explanation left Aryiah wondering why she would need the ability to monitor her Witches, but before she could speak her question, Yuna stepped back into the room and bowed. "Goddess, the ceremony is about to begin."

Aryiah's nervousness immediately returned, slamming into her like a runaway train. Completing her rites had been a piece of cake, but facing the entire realm of Ovialell was something she didn't think she'd ever be ready to do. Not to mention her impending wedding.

"Just breathe," the goddess instructed.

Aryiah did just that as she followed her mother down to the throne room through a winding staircase that led to the back side of the dais. There was a large curtain surrounding the area, and two elaborately carved chairs sat side by side. Though Aryiah hadn't seen her mother grab her Book of Shadows, it now rested on a small table between the chairs.

Diana gestured for her to take her place, so Aryiah walked forward and sat in the chair. She didn't see Damarius or any of the Witches, but she could make out the mumbling of throngs of people on the other side of the curtain.

Once seated in the opposite throne, Diana reached for her hand. "Are you ready?"

All she could do was nod her head.

CHAPTER FORTY-ONE

The curtain surrounding them fell away, and Aryiah suddenly found herself staring at the faces of hundreds, if not thousands of people.

Struck by the beauty of the room, she took a moment to look around. The white marble columns sparkled in the fairy lights that floated in the air. She's knew what they were from Aradia's memories, but had never seen anything like them before as Aryiah. The balls of light floated around the room of their own accord in hues she'd never seen.

The rustle of the crowd caused her eyes to drop back to the floor. She then noticed a blood red carpet runner that split the large crowd in half. Gazing to the left, she immediately found her Witches gathered at the front of the crowd, all grinning wildly in her direction. Her vision then moved across the room and locked onto a group of massive warrior-type men standing on the opposite side. The connection she felt after one look told Aryiah that these were her wolves. In unison, they nodded in her direction; Aryiah kindly tilted her head in response. They all smiled at her acknowledgement, and suddenly she couldn't wait to get to know each and every one of them.

Before Aryiah could scan the rest of the crowd, Diana stood, commanding everyone's attention with her presence alone. She wore a purple gown made of the same silk as Aryiah's wedding dress. It crisscrossed in front, as most of the goddess' garments did, and her trademark silver belt hung from her hips.

"Thank you for joining me on this joyous occasion." Her voice radiated power and carried throughout the room as if magnified by an unseen microphone.

"Today, I have glorious news. Aradia has returned! My daughter has been reincarnated in Aryiah and has reclaimed her place as the Queen of the Witches."

The crowd let out a hesitant cheer that made Aryiah want to sink down in her chair until she was no longer the target of hundreds of doubting eyes.

"Behold! Aradia has awakened and returned to save us once more. She has defeated the vampire assassin that has been plaguing our realm," the goddess declared grandly. "Please welcome Aryiah to our world as she accepts her rightful place by my side."

As Diana handed her the Book of Shadows, all Aryiah could think of was making her escape. Her thoughts focused on her favorite dessert as she tried to calm herself enough to face this judgmental crowd. Her nerves spiked again as she looked around and thought, *Maybe I'm not ready to take my rightful place. How is this even possible?*

The desire to shade out of here overwhelmed her. The idea of returning earth-side and leaving all this behind sounded like a great plan. But no, instead, she now sat in the throne room holding the book that announced to all of Ovialell who she truly was.

As she gazed at the hordes of unfamiliar faces her stomach tighten and her entire body started to shake. But suddenly, she felt a strong hand settle on her shoulder. Damarius' touch alone was enough to calm her nerves. The only problem was, his nearness also stirred the wolf she was now able to become.

"My love, I am barely in control right now."

He chuckled quietly, then sent his thoughts into her mind. *"I'm sorry to have rustled your wolf, but listening to your musings about chocolate crème pie and the thought of you licking it from my chest has left me ravenous. I think I'll be reminding you of the idea later."*

A smile spread across Aryiah's face. With this sexy man beside her, she knew she was ready to accept her destiny.

Aryiah stood and lifted the now glowing book above her head and the crowd went wild.

EPILOGUE

Devin watched as Aryiah held a glowing book above her head, and listened as the crowd began to cheer.

When she heard the goddess announce that her precious Aradia had returned and eliminated the vampire assassin, it had taken every ounce of her willpower not to fly out from behind the stone pillar and start ripping out throats until she was soaked in blood and holding Aryiah's heart in her hand.

The only thing that held her back was the humor she found in the fact that they all truly believed this was over. Little did they know that when Aryiah destroyed Gage with Aradia's magick, she inadvertently made Devin practically unstoppable.

The Darkling had been right. The bond she and Gage shared had indeed been special. The loss she felt as Aryiah destroyed her lover had threatened to overwhelm her in the moment, but when she realized that Gage's dark magick was now hers, and that they'd always be connected through it, she steeled her resolve.

While Aryiah had stood there demanding she leave and never return, the shock she had felt wasn't from her previous friend's words, but from the surge of magick that had flowed into her at the moment of Gage's death.

So, let them have their party and celebrate, because soon enough . . . she would have her revenge.

Places and Settings:

Ovialell – Pronounced (Oh-Vee-uh-lell) The "Otherworld" ruled by the Goddess Diana and protected by her Witches.

Shadowlands – The alternate realm in which those with the ability to shade use to travel from place to place.

Dalestri– Pronounced (Da-les-tri) Home of the Goddess Diana, the werewolves, and the Witches on the Upper World of Ovialell.

Themiscyra – Pronounced (Them-is-cyra) Home of the Amazons. An island off the northern shore of Dalestri on the Upper World of Ovialell.

Inlavey – Home of the Seelie Fae in the Middle World of Ovialell.

Karistan – Home of the Unseelie Fae in the Middle World of Ovialell.

Obsidian – Home of the vampires in the Lower World of Ovialell.

Hel – Home of the demons in the Lower World of Ovialell.

Races and Organizations:

The Witches – A coven of powerful witches who run with the Goddess Diana during the Wild Hunt, and are charged with protecting the citizens of Ovialell with their magick and healing abilities.

Werewolves – A race created for the specific purpose of protecting the goddess, and who run with her during the Wild Hunt. Led by Damarius.

Darklings – A humanoid race of creatures with extensive magickal powers and a thirst for destruction. Responsible for starting the war referred to as the Great Rift.

Amazons – A race of magically enhanced women who live on the Island of Themiscyra. They are fierce warriors and support the Goddess Diana. Led by Kylie.

The Seelie Fae – A race of light Fae, known for their playful ways, white magick, intricate carvings, and magickal land. Led by Queen Shay.

The Unseelie Fae – A race of dark Fae, known for their twisted land and dark magic. Led by Queen Fayln.

Vampires – Simple creatures of death that feed on human blood, enjoy the kill, and lurk in the night.

Demons – Considered the worst creatures of Ovialell for their infighting and scavenger-like destruction; Demons are humanoid creatures with transparent flesh stretched over emaciated skeletons, giving them the appearance of being see-through, with their longs arms ending in pointed claws instead of fingers.

Phrases and Terms:

Shading – The ability to travel through the Shadowlands from one place to another while remaining shaded and hidden from the rest of the world.

The Great Rift – A war started by the Darklings which divided Ovialell between good and evil, ending in a horrible loss of life and destruction.

Shamanic Journey – A series of meditative journeys that a Witch is led through by her guide. The shamanic journeys start in Lower World, then up to Middle World, and finally to Upper World, where they meet the goddess. During these journeys they not only face trials, but are given instructions on what they should be studying in the real world in order to prepare them for the release of their magick.

A Rite of Passage, a Dangerous Trial,
a Destiny to be Claimed.

Please turn this page for a preview of

Shay and the Box of Nye

~An Ovialell Companion ~

CHAPTER ONE

Shay jumped from her bed and ran to the calendar that hung on the wall of her room. December twenty-fourth. She stared at the date, double checking to make sure it wasn't just wishful thinking.

"Yes!"

She ran from her bedroom, her gauzy blue nightgown billowing behind her as she made her way down the small spiral staircase that led to the kitchen.

"Mama, my trial starts today. I'm so nervous." She sat down at the table and scooped herself a portion of berry and cinnamon oatmeal from the large pot in front of her, then continued. "Can you give me some hints or tell me what yours was like?"

"Don't be nervous, Shay. The fairy trial is something every mature fairy has to go through. I can't tell you anything about my trial though, because if you're successful in retrieving the

203

Box of Nye, part of the process is that the memories of what you faced during your trial are completely erased. This happens as you receive your wings and complete the transformation into a full-fledge fairy."

"Really? You don't remember anything at all about your trial?"

"No, honey. I sure don't." Narine turned off the stove and took a seat next to her oldest daughter. "Just follow the rules, and prepare for the unexpected." She kissed Shay on the forehead and moved to exit the room. "I'll leave you alone to get ready. The fairy council will be here shortly to go over everything. Good luck, honey. I know you'll do great."

Shay finished her oatmeal as she pondered her mother's words, *"Prepare for the unexpected."*

"How the heck are you supposed to do that?" The whole point of something being unexpected is that you *can't* prepare for it. This definitely didn't help put her mind at ease, but she knew dwelling on the what ifs wasn't an option. She placed her wooden bowl in the sink and headed back upstairs to get ready for the council's arrival.

As she entered her bedroom a feeling of peace settled over her. She was so grateful she finally had a space to herself—one that she didn't have to share with her younger sisters any more. When Shay reached maturity at the age of eighteen, her mom and dad had used their fairy magick to expand their treetop home, creating a beautiful bedroom and bathroom just for her. The ceiling was lined with vines and fairy lights, and crystals of all colors shined from their facets in the walls.

Shay stared at her reflection in the mirror as the tub began to fill, she noticed her skin was shimmering a little brighter than usual, and her long platinum hair was starting to develop streaks of blue and silver throughout. Looking into her own sapphire eyes, she smiled. The process of becoming a full-fledge fairy had already begun.

Each fairy develops a specific set of magick during their transformation, and as Shay stared at the blue and silver steaks weaving their way through her hair, she couldn't have been happier. Blue meant that she'd be able to control water and emotions, and silver was a link to their Queen and the divine fairy spirits. Silver was rare magick within their clan, and meant someday she would have the potential of becoming Queen, as only those with silver magick had the necessary link to the fairy spirits required to take a royal position.

Shay slipped off her nightgown and stepped into the steaming bath, allowing herself to appreciate the relaxing lavender aroma that was a constant in any bathroom across the land. If you ran water in a kitchen it always smelled like citrus. If you ran water outside it smelled like fresh cut grass even if it was the dead of winter. But here in the bathroom it was always lavender laced.

Taking the time to let her muscles relax, Shay started to make a mental list of all the things she'd planned to take with her on the trial. Her leather vest, riding pants, and tall boots would be her chosen outfit, which was traditional. However, she planned to include a few extra things into the belt and pockets she'd added to her ensemble. Things like her favorite knife which was made from tampered steel that displayed a polished finish of rainbow colors. And the spell bottle she carried like a canteen which was a beautiful mix of blue, green, and purple glass. It was now filled to the brim with the potion she recently brewed for this specific day. For reasons beyond her understanding, she'd been guided in its creation and knew it was going to be something she'd need.

Shay had been dreaming of and preparing for this day for most of her teenage years but now that it was upon her, she couldn't help but wonder if she'd done enough.

A Demon Queen, a Blessed Child,

a Battle that begins History.

Please turn this page for a preview of

Prophecy's Child

~An Ovialell Companion ~

CHAPTER ONE

Kylie's throat was on fire. She literally couldn't scream anymore. The moment the demons entered her home, she tried to grab her little sister and flee, but she just wasn't fast enough.

"Don't worry about the little one," one of the demons said. "She's too young to enter the breeding program. But you . . . you'll do just fine." The menace in his voice had Kylie screaming through the pain of her raw vocal cords.

After dragging her outside, the demons threw her into the back of the transport carriage, which was nothing more than a metal cage on the back of an old wooden wagon. Once she righted herself, she took in the faces of the other sobbing women. There was Trina, the blacksmith's daughter, and her cousin Lucy, along with Avetta, the storekeeper's wife, and Reni, the stablemaster's sister.

Kylie kept a cautious eye on the guards as they made their way to the front of the carriage. Once she was sure they were out of earshot, she turned to the women. "Don't be afraid. I'll do everything within my power to get us out of here." The girls looked at her with hope blooming in their eyes, then immediately dried their tears. They knew that if anyone could save them it would be Kylie.

Kylie was twenty-three and had *matured* years ago. With her long dark hair and tall slender figure, she was a perfect candidate for the breeding program. She grew up hearing stories of the evil queen and her red-eyed demons from Abrinthill. They roamed the three realms, gathering female prisoners in order to continue their race, but they'd never set foot in her realm . . . until now.

Luckily for the women, Kylie wasn't the average prisoner. She had powers that no one else in the village had had for over five-hundred years. Her village sat on an ancient vortex of magick, one that the former spirit women utilized to sustain the prosperity of their land.

It was foretold that once every five-hundred years, a new spirit woman would be born in order to continue the magickal workings. When Kylie was born, the priests divined that she would be the village's next spirit woman. Once they verified she bore the mark of the prophecy's child—a crescent moon on the inside of her thigh—they waited until her thirteenth birthday to begin her training, as was customary.

The priests didn't possess any magick, but were educated in how to prepare the blessed women for their duties. The old texts that guided them in the ancient ways were kept secret in the catacomb library of the abandoned church. The books' location was passed down from generation to generation.

Once Kylie had been properly trained in the ways of her magick, she ventured to the lowest level of the abandoned church where she bathed in the Spring of Spirits. There, she completed the ritual to seal her powers and become the current prophecy's child.

As Kylie's home was being raided, on the other side of the village, Rezmona entered the church. She expected to hear screams, but instead was met with silence.

"Where's Gregor?" she snapped.

The guards on duty stood at attention. "My Queen. Gregor said to let you know we are in the process of moving the prisoners."

That explained the silence, but not the reason behind it. The deserted church had served as a good base of operations for months now.

"I believe you'll find him in, um . . . in the office," the other guard stuttered. His eyes found the floor as he shifted nervously on his feet.

Rezmona's stare bore into him for a fraction of a second, then she headed towards the office without giving a response. The guard exhaled a sigh of relief.

The hall, with its moss-covered walls and heavy wooden doors, was bathed in flickering candlelight. Rezmona recognized the feelings of homesickness, but quickly shut them down. If they were moving the prisoners, returning home wasn't something that was going to happen anytime soon.

Rezmona was the demon queen of Abrinthill, the largest and most lavish city in all of the realms. She was beautiful, but also the most brutal queen that had ever ruled.

She had long black hair, a shapely figure, plump ruby lips, and blood red eyes. But along with her gothic inspired skirts and corsets, her appearance was only an illusion she cast. A demon's true nature was only revealed when they shed their glamour, which they didn't do often. However, on the rare occasion they did, their true form was that of large, red-skinned towering beasts. They wore no clothes, which left them naked and exposed, and each with a set of horns which protruded from their heads.

When Rezmona claimed her natural form, her horns were stunning. Shiny black with gold stripes running through them, resembling a tiger's eye stone. They curved and spiraled into perfect points, which truly made her a sight to behold in either form. As the queen, she was also the only female demon whose eyes still glowed red and who was allowed to travel outside their city of Abrinthill.

Centuries ago, the females of their race suddenly began to lose the color of their eyes. Panic ensued when it was soon discovered they were no longer able to reproduce. The only explanation the elders offered was that their race was being punished by the Gods for constantly reproducing with world domination being their only goal.

At the time, the only blessing was that the queen's eyes had retained their natural hue. With the help of her mentors, she'd perfected the dark magick needed to continue their race, although at a much slower pace. The breeding program was founded, and ever since, the continuation of their existence solely depended upon impregnating the prisoners they collected from across the three realms.

The last time Rezmona and her demons made one of these gathering trips, they'd gained over sixteen new prisoners—each fertile and ready to enter the breeding program. Although the program was a success, it didn't change the fact that leaving her palace was something she never looked forward to.

When Rezmona entered the church office she found Gregor hunched over the desk reading from a tattered old book. "Gregor, what is the meaning of this? Why are we moving the prisoners?"

He took a moment to mark his place, then looked up at her with tired eyes. "Just a precaution, my Queen. We have stayed here for far too long, and if we plan to collect more prisoners, we had better move now, before their loved ones attempt a rescue."

Easing her way across the room with a serious look on her

face, Rezmona suddenly slammed her hands down on the old wooden desk. "That is no reason to move the prisoners! I could crush anyone who attempted such a foolish mission. Now, what's the real reason we are leaving, and what is it that you're reading?"

Gregor, her mentor, had served her mother and grandmother before her. He wore a long hooded robe to conceal his weathered face, because even under his glamour, age had clearly left its mark on this centuries-old demon. He walked with a tall wooden staff, presenting an image of an old and feeble demonic monk. But just as his appearance was an illusion, so was that assumption. Gregor's magick was extremely powerful, and in his prime, he was considered one of the most vile men in Abrinthill.

He squinted slightly, then gathered the book into his robe. "Just an old manuscript regarding the history of the town and its people. I found it here in the church."

Gregor was known to be a history buff so this shouldn't seem out of the ordinary. Seeming to relax ever so slightly, she asked, "Have you learned anything of value from it?"

"Nothing extraordinary. The church was founded over three thousand years ago. The people of the village lived modestly, and their town has always been very prosperous." Gregor motioned for her to follow him out the door.

"Prosperity is good. Hopefully that will translate to the fertility of their women as well," Rezmona replied, then

217

followed her mentor to the carriage waiting at the back of the church.

"And to answer your previous question, my Queen, the main reason I've decided to move the prisoners has to do with the amount of time we'll be staying. I know how much you hate having to leave Abrinthill, so my plan is to gather enough prisoners this trip to sustain the breeding program for at least a solid year. If that goal is met, we would soon run out of room here in the church," Gregor explained. "I've started moving the prisoners to the abandoned castle on the outskirts of town. Even though the transport from the village will take longer, the castle will serve as a good base of operations until we are ready to return home."

Rezmona remembered the castle he was referring to. She'd noticed it during their initial trip into town. The back of it literally hung over a cliff, and the front was easily defended. He was right . . . it would serve as a perfect base. As she entered the carriage the idea of not having to leave Abrinthill for over a year put a smile on her face. "Continue dealing with the prisoners, Gregor. I'll meet you at the castle when you're done."

* * * * *

Gregor hadn't heard Rezmona approaching the office, so when she caught him reading from the ancient text, it had indeed startled him. And though her questioning his motives had set his teeth on edge, he quickly diffused the queen's anger with his even-keeled response, because he wasn't ready to discuss what he'd found within the manuscript just yet. At present, he was only a quarter way through the book, but due to his powers of foresight knew it was important to finish it as soon as possible.

The day they'd entered the town, he'd been immediately drawn to this church, and after weeks of searching the ruins, he found the tattered book buried deep within its catacomb library. The moment he held it in his hands, he sensed it was imperative to gain the knowledge within, but the question of why still remained.

ABOUT THE AUTHOR

Bestselling and Award-Winning Author, Tish Thawer, writes paranormal romances for all ages. From her first paranormal cartoon, Isis, to the Twilight phenomenon, myth, magic, and superpowers have always held a special place in her heart.

Tish is known for her detailed world-building and magic-laced stories. Her work has been compared to Nora Roberts, Sam Cheever, and Charlaine Harris. She has received nominations for a RONE Award (Reward of Novel Excellence), and Author of the Year (Fantasy, Dystopian, Mystery), as well as nominations and wins for Best Cover, and Reader's Choice Award.

Tish has worked as a computer consultant, photographer, and graphic designer, and is a columnist for Gliterary Girl media and has bylines in RT Magazine and Literary Lunes Magazine. She resides in Arizona with her husband and three wonderful children and is represented by Gandolfo, Helin, and Fountain Literary Management.

You can find out more about Tish and her all titles by visiting: www.TishThawer.com and subscribing to her newsletter at www.tishthawer.com/subscribe

The Rose Trilogy
Scent of a White Rose - Book 1
Roses & Thorns - Book 1.5
Blood of a Red Rose - Book 2
Death of a Black Rose - Book 3

The Ovialell Series
Prophecy's Child - Companion
The Rise of Rae - Companion
Shay and the Box of Nye - Companion
Behind the Veil - Omnibus
Dark Seeds - Book 1.5

The Women of Purgatory
Raven's Breath - Book 1
Dark Abigail - Book 2

The Witches of BlackBrook
The Witches of BlackBrook - Book 1
The Daughters of Maine - Book 2

The TS901 Chronicles
TS901:Anomaly - Book 1

Collections
Christmas Lites II
Losing It: A Collection of V-Cards
Fairy Tale Confessions
Dance With Me

.

Made in the USA
Lexington, KY
07 November 2017